Suddenly, over all the sounds of marine
engines and the rushing of the
sea, I heard her tormented cries:
"Bastards!" she yelled at the top of her
lungs. "Bastards, bastards, bastards!"
The sound came from amidships.
I swung my ankles into the light and
sawed feebly at the exposed wire.
It parted after an anguished eternity.
When I had pulled the sickening
cloth out of my mouth, I tried to stand and
went sprawling. Both feet were
numbed. I pulled myself up and stood
in the semidarkness, holding onto
the rail, stamping my feet, trying to
bring the feeling back to them.
"Stop!" I could hear her scream.
"Oh God! Stop!"
I tested my weight on feet that felt
like wooden paddles. My hands
hung like sacks of putty. I tried to move
fast, hoping for surprise, knowing
I had no time left . . .

Where Is Janice Gantry?

JOHN D. MacDONALD

FAWCETT GOLD MEDAL • NEW YORK

WHERE IS JANICE GANTRY?

Published by Fawcett Gold Medal Books, a unit of CBS Publications, the Consumer Publishing Division of CBS Inc.

Copyright © 1961 by John D. MacDonald

ISBN: 0-449-14224-8

Printed in the United States of America

17   16   15   14   13   12   11   10   9

Chapter One

SOMETIMES the hot night wind brings bad dreams. It came streaming and steaming out of the west, piling the Gulf into a continual rumble of freight trains along the beach of Horseshoe Key, whipping the water of the wide bay inside the Key, and galloping along to rip and clatter the fronds of the cabbage palms beside my mainland cottage, to excite a squeaking and groaning of bamboo, to hiss and sigh through the tall Australian pines.

I slept deep in a heartbreak dream of the girl that was lost and gone, of my wife Judy, no longer mine, no longer wife. In my dream I looked out of blackness into a lighted room where she smiled upon a faceless man the way she had always smiled at me. I bellowed and pounded on the thick glass between us but she could not hear me. Or would not.

I came bursting up out of the dream, tense, sweaty, wide-awake, searching through all the turmoil of the west wind for some sound that did not fit the night. There was moonlight, coming and going between a scud of clouds. The curtain whipped and writhed in the moonlight. I did not know what I listened for until it came again, a sly scratching against the copper screening three feet from my head.

I slid open the bottom drawer of the night stand, reached into the back of it and fumbled the oily cloth open to take the gun into my hand, feeling more assured but self-consciously dramatic, remembering the last time I had used it, months ago, to pot a palm tree rat eating from the bird feeder. It was loaded, as guns should always be. As I rolled off the bed toward the window, one knee against the harshness of the rattan matting, the scratching sound came again, and this time I heard the voice almost lost in the wind sounds, hoarse, urgent, cautious, speaking my name.

"Sam! Sam Brice!"

As I angled closer to look out, the moon was suddenly gone. "Who is it?"

"It's Charlie, Sam. Charlie Haywood. Let me in. Don't turn on any lights, Sam."

I went through the small living room and out onto the screened porch and unhooked the door and let him in. I smelled him when he went by me into the dark living room. He stank of the swamps, of sweat and panic and flight.

"Something I can sit on, Sam? I'm a mess. I don't want to ruin anything." His voice was a half whisper, and I could sense the exhaustion in him.

He sat in a straight chair near the kitchen alcove, sighing as he sat down. "You know about me, Sam?"

"I read the papers. You've been news for five days, Charlie."

"They making any guesses, about where I am?"

"The dogs tracked you south from the road camp before they lost you. They think you're heading for the keys."

"Those goddam dogs! I circled back, Sam, after I bitched up those goddam dogs. I didn't know if it would work. An old-timer told me it would. A pint bottle of gas I drained out of one of the trucks. When I got to a piece of open water big enough, I spread it thick on the shore where I went in. They snuff that, it's supposed to put them out of business for an hour. I did some swimming, Sam. My God, I did some swimming. Have you got any cold milk? A bottle of it. I've been thinking about cold milk ever since I can remember."

I thumbed the top off a new bottle and handed it to him, and sat near him, hearing the sound of his thirst.

"My God, that's good! I'd forgotten how good."

I went back into the bedroom and stowed the gun away and looked at the luminous dial of my alarm clock. Twenty after three.

6

When I turned he was close to me, startling me.

"I wouldn't want you to use the phone, Sam."

Anger was quick. "You made the choice, boy. You came to me. If you figured it wrong, it's too late now, isn't it? If I'm going to turn you in, you can't stop me."

"I'm sorry," he said humbly. "I'm not thinking very good, Sam."

We went back and sat and he finished the milk.

"Nice of you," I said, "to count me in on this. It's just what I need."

"Don't be sore, Sam."

"I didn't know we're such close friends, buddy."

"I went through the list fifty times, Sam, and it always came out to be you."

"Why?"

"I knew I'd have to have help from somebody. I had to take the chance you'd still be living out here, a place I thought I could get to, and still living alone, Sam. I knew you wouldn't scare easy. And, working for yourself, you've got more freedom to move around. And I don't know if you remember it, but one time you hinted about the dirty deal you got—just enough so I guess you know how it feels to . . . get sent up for something you didn't do. The way you feel so helpless."

"For something you didn't do!"

"I know how that sounds, Sam."

"It sounds as if you'd lost your mind, boy."

On the basis of all the known facts, Charlie Haywood was going to have all kinds of trouble peddling that story. Over two years ago he had been a car salesman at the Mel Fifer Agency here in Florence City, and the business I own and operate had brought me in contact with him. He was a reasonably likeable kid, about 23, a little too dreamy and mild to be a very good car salesman, but, because he lived with his widowed mother who had a small income and also rented rooms to tourists, he didn't have to make much to get along. I'd had a few beers with him several times and cased him as one of those optimistic, idealistic kids who, if he could find a bride with enough drive and guts, might find enough on the ball to make himself a tidy happy life.

7

And I guess it flattered me a little to be with him because he hadn't recovered from the fact that I was one of his childhood heroes. When he had been in grade school I'd been Sam Brice, fullback, the big ground-gainer in the West Coast Florida Conference, with offers from every semi-pro college team in the East. And he was willing to forget that out of my own arrogance and stupidity I had let the wide world whip me and I had come home after three seasons with the National Football League with my tail tucked down and under.

Anyway, as the newspapers had brought out, Charlie Haywood had been acting gloomy and erratic for several weeks before he got in the jam. He drove out onto Horseshoe Key late one March afternoon, broke into the luxurious beach residence of a Mr. Maurice Weber, who had recently been a customer of the Fifer Agency, and had been apprehended while trying to pry loose a wall safe set into the rear wall of a bedroom closet. Mr. Weber had found him there, had held a gun on him, disarmed him and called the Sheriff's office.

Charlie had spent three weeks in the County Jail awaiting the next session of the Circuit Court. He pleaded guilty and was sentenced to five years. I heard that after a short indoctrination period at Raiford Prison, he had been transferred to one of the state road camps down in the 'Glades.

Though he had been gone over twenty-eight months, I could remember the gossip at the time he was sent up—how Weber had paid for a new car with cash, so it was possible there was more cash at the house. They said Charlie had been drinking a little too much, and his performance had been so poor the sales manager had warned him to straighten out or be fired.

"I haven't lost my mind, Sam. I pleaded guilty. I had to. I couldn't tell the whole story. It was the only thing I could do. I mean that was the way it seemed at the time. But . . . I've had a lot of time to think. And one day, a month ago, it all seemed to come together in my mind, all the loose parts of it, and I knew I'd been the worst damn fool the world has ever seen, and I knew I had to get out and come back here."

8

"And do what?"

"Prove it was all lies, everything she said to me."

"Who?"

"Charity Weber. The hell with bringing you into all that, Sam. It's my problem. I've got to do it my own way."

"What do you want from me?"

"I want clothes and sleep and a chance to get clean. Nobody will ever know I was here, Sam. I swear I won't tell anybody. I'm in terrible shape right now, but I'll come back fast. They did one thing for me, Sam. They made me tough enough, mentally and physically, for what I've got to do. That guy you used to know, Sam. He doesn't exist any more."

"This puts me in a hell of a spot."

"I know that. I didn't tell you one of the reasons I came here. It's because I'd do the same thing for you."

There is no good answer to that statement.

After a long pause I said, "Okay, Charlie. But I wish I knew more about all this."

"All you have to know is I give you my word I'm not guilty. And the reason I said I was is because . . . if it would have helped her in any little way to stick my hand in a fire, I would have held it there and grinned while it roasted. I'd had a good big taste of her and I would have died for her—and she knew it and so did he—so five years seemed like a little favor, something I was anxious to do. I wasn't . . . equipped to handle a woman like that."

His words brought Judy back into my mind, so vividly I knew she had been in my dreams in all the windy night.

I had a commitment I did not want, and I could smell the trouble coming; but I told myself it would be entirely reasonable to let him get the rest he needed, so that when he was himself again, I could quietly talk him into letting me call Sheriff Pat Millhaus to come and get him.

The bathroom light did not alarm him, so while he showered and used my razor, I put on pants and sneakers and carried the foul wad of his prison clothing and ruined shoes out behind the garage to a corner out of the wind, dug a hole in the loose, sandy soil, buried the stuff deep and stomped the soil flat. I tossed a pair of my pajamas into the bathroom. I was making up the spare bed in my

9

bedroom when he came back out.

There was a first gray of dawn in the room, just enough so that I could see him for the first time. He had been slender, with a round boyish face. He was leaned down to emaciation, his face drawn tight against sharp bones. Road work in the tropic sun had tanned him deeply. His face was scabbed, lumped, welted by the swamp insects that had bitten him during his flight, and his eyes were drowsy. He sat on the bed and said, "Made it. More than a hundred miles across that crazy empty country. Sloughs and hammocks and saw-grass." He lay back and pulled the sheet and the single cotton blanket up, sighed deeply, and went to sleep.

I tried to sleep but I knew there was no chance. I dressed and made coffee and drank it out on the screened porch. The wind was beginning to die, and suddenly it stopped entirely just as the sun was coming up. In the stillness, the muggy heat was like a stale blanket. I heard a sudden thrash of water down near my dock, and I snatched the spinner and trotted down the path and saw the swirl of some snook working twenty feet out. It was the middle of August, when they work the passes and the bays by moonlight, and these boys were on their way home, with room for a final snack. I dropped the white bucktail a dozen feet beyond them and began yanking it back through the swirls, and it banged hard just when I hoped it would be. Had he scooted under the dock, as too many of them have done, his only damage would have been a sore mouth. But he took off toward open water. I had six pound test, but a lot of it, so he finally turned, losing a little steam, and I walked forty feet down the narrow beach, bringing him back, watching him show twice in the golden slant of the early sun, checking his rushes, finally gentling him up onto the rough broken shell of the narrow bay beach, his gills working, his eyes big as dimes. I saw he would go around ten, maybe a little over. After I had clubbed him and picked him up and was sure of him, I realized that a wolf pack of mosquitoes had found me, and I remembered again that I was entertaining a house guest who was being hunted by every law officer in the state of Florida.

10

After I had rinsed the rod, cleaned the fish and put him in the small refrigerator, and washed up, I did a few chores and wrote a note to leave for Charlie Haywood. "I've locked the place up. I've laid out clothes that should fit you. Look around and you'll find orange juice, coffee etc. There's eggs, milk, bacon, fresh-caught snook in the ice box. Help yourself. Nobody is likely to come here during the day. I'll make it back in the middle of the afternoon."

I had laid out a brown knit sport shirt that had been too small for me from the day I bought it, and some khaki pants that had shrunk too small.

After I locked the cottage behind me, I drove the four miles north into Florence City. It was Monday morning, the 15th day of August, getting stickier and hotter every minute. After I got my mail out of my box at the post office, I drove on out across City Bridge to the commercial area adjacent to Orange Beach, parked my old Ford ranch wagon behind the office and walked across the street to Cy's Lunch and Sundries for breakfast.

"You early as can be, Sambo," he said.

"It's Monday, Cyrus. New week. New start. Energy. Git up and go."

"Oh, sure," he said sourly, busting my two eggs onto the grill.

I found one small story on the Haywood escape on the lower half of the third page. They were still looking for him. They expected to recapture him any minute. There was a possibility he had stolen a car in Clewiston and abandoned it in Tampa.

When I walked back to the office after breakfast, Sis Gantry had arrived and opened it up. The big rackety air conditioner was just beginning to make its chilly function felt. Actually the cinderblock structure is the place of business of Tom Earle, Realtor. It has one big room, with his private office and the wash rooms and storage room behind it, in the rear. There are seven desks in the big room, with six of them used by his associates and his clerical help, and one of them rented to me. I am Automotive Appraisal Associates, which is an overly impressive name for a one-man firm. The monthly figure I pay him covers desk space, phone service (including phone answering service by his gals when I am out) and the right to have my name in small print, along with the name of my business, painted on the bottom half of the front door.

Sis Gantry faked vast surprise and said, "I get it! That crummy shack of yours must have burned down."

"My good woman, I caught and cleaned a snook this morning before your alarm went off."

Her name is Janice, but she is never called anything except Sis. She is a local girl with eight brothers, four older and four younger, so it is a fate she could hardly escape. She is a big-boned brunette, full of life and bounce and sparkle, a truly warmhearted person. She has a wide hearty mouth, a strikingly good figure—firm, rounded and ample—and very dark blue eyes.

Sis and I will never be at ease with each other. It started in the wrong way with us, and after a while it became obvious it should never have started at all. I met her nearly four years ago. They had whipped me and I had come back to my home town, knowing I should give a damn about what happened to the rest of my life, but finding it hard to care. I had been in town a month and I was doing rough carpentry work for one of the local builders when I met her. She was just getting over being whipped. She was twenty-five then, and I was a year older. She had made one of those impossible marriages, to a wild man— psychotic, alcoholic, vicious. A girl with less optimism and vitality than Sis would have gotten out of it in the first year. But she stuck it out for four childless, incredible years, until he shot her in the throat and himself in the roof of the mouth. She survived only because there was a very good man on the ambulance.

We were a couple of prominent misfits in Florence City, and we joined forces and talked out our problems to each other. She had to have a project, because it helped her keep her mind off her own problems, and she elected me. It was due to her prodding that I began to look seriously for some kind of work that would suit me. Old Bert Shilder at the Central Bank and Trust, who had known my parents all their lives right up until they drowned in the Gulf in a storm fifteen years ago, put me onto this accident appraisal business and got me a job with a firm over in Miami. After four months I knew enough about the business to take the chance of starting up on my own in Florence City.

It was Sis Gantry who applauded the decision, reviewed my precarious finances, decided I should own a place rather than rent, and found the old cottage on the bay shore on one acre of overgrown land four miles south of the city line. She was working for Tom Earle by then, and she knew it was a steal and, after she had bullied me into it, she felt she had earned the right to help me fix it up. And it was Sis who wangled the desk space in Tom Earle's beach office for me.

Up until about two weeks after I had moved into the cottage, sex had had no place in our relationship. We were friends and we'd both had a bad time, and we were able to relax with each other. Then one Sunday evening she brought over the kitchen curtains she had made. I put the fixtures up and she hung curtains. October thunder came banging down along the keys, and then the rain came swamping down and the electricity went off. We made bad jokes about it. There were no candles back then, and no flashlight. We sat on the couch. I could see her in every blue-white flicker of lightning. I was reaching for the cigarettes when I happened to touch her hand. I closed my fingers around her waist. At the next flash of lightning I saw her face, inches from mine, eyes shadowy wide and lips apart. A few moments after the kiss began she was straining for a greater closeness, her mouth heated, her breath fast and shallow. She suffered herself to be led into the bedroom, docile as a child, and she turned this way and that way to aid me as, with hands made clumsy by a vast urgency, I undressed her there.

I had had no one since Judy, and she had had no one since that madman who had put the dimpled scar in the side of her throat.

For the many weeks after that, through the end of that year and into the next year, it was a lopsidedly sexual relationship, and all of it took place in that cottage, screened from the road and the neighbors by the wildness of the untended brush. It was a strong, obsessive and

13

joyous thing. There was no coyness, no teasing, no parlor games. It never seemed to take more than thirty seconds from the doorway to the bed, in unvarying readiness. We were both husky vital people, and there was always time for laughter and for bawdy foolish jokes about our capacities for this joyful, single-minded game. We padded about in a comfortable nudity, cooking and devouring huge meals. As she lived with her family, she felt she had to spend a portion of each night in her own bed. But more often than not I would be awakened in the morning by Sis, arriving, stripping, lunging into my bed to snuffle and giggle into my throat, with busy hands and busy lips.

I do not know exactly why it ended. I think it began partly because she wanted to cure me of Judy, as one more segment of her project to bring me back into the human race.

Pehaps it ended because she was not content to stop there. She wanted more. Maybe she wanted marriage. It was never mentioned. But she began to prod me. The first thing she wanted me to do was all too obvious. I was settling too snugly into a small occupation, and it was clear to her that I wanted to keep it small. I had long since given up the luxury of ambition. I wanted something that would support me and not make too many demands.

By luck I had found just what I wanted. A batch of major automobile insurance companies employed me on a fee basis. Insurance adjustors and lawyers would handle the liability aspects of each accident. It was my job to appraise the physical damage to the vehicles so that claims could be equitably adjusted. I had to keep the greedy claimant from getting a complete body job out of one dinged fender, but I also tried to make certain the insurance company involved paid for all the damage arising out of the particular accident where their policy holder was at fault. The more fair, impartial and objective I could be, the better I could do my job.

During each tourist season I worked long rugged hours. That was when the folks from Ohio and Indiana and Michigan were down, leaping at each other with a great clashing of tail fins and gnashing of grill work. I could pile up enough in those months to see me nicely through the reduced income and lazy hours of the rest of the year.

But Sis kept working on me. I should go out and dig for more business. Maybe I should get into more adjusting. Line up more client companies. Hire another man when it got to be more than I could handle. Expand, grow, become important. Pile up the profit and reinvest it in land.

As the bedroom extravagances began to slow to a less lurid pace, she became more insistent on guiding my Future. But I had exactly what I wanted, and all I wanted. I had food, shelter, clothing, tobacco and liquor sufficient to my needs. I had time off to catch snook, hunt wild turkey, walk on the beach. I was content to ride with just what I had for all the rest of the distance. I couldn't make her see that.

The other thing she wanted was less obvious. I am not certain she could have put it into words. But she wanted more emotional response from me. She wanted the words and looks and actions of immortal love. And it just wasn't there to give to anybody. I had given it once, to Judy. She had walked away with it. So I could only use Sis. I could take my pleasure in the ultimate use of that sturdy eager body, and find my rationalization in those gasps and archings and moanings that told me the pleasure I was giving equalled what I was taking, but I could not go beyond that specific and obvious act into my area or faked area of love undying, even though I sensed that that was what she needed and wanted.

For a period of weeks I was able to endure the nagging, direct and indirect, for the sake of the bounty of having her in my bed, but after a time the balance shifted and it was no longer worth it. I made a few clumsy excuses and she stopped arriving unannounced. I asked her out to the cottage a few more times, and she came willingly, but something indefinable had gone out of it, some aspect of joy and freedom. We went through the motions and assured each other it was all just great, but it wasn't.

There was no scene, no wild and bitter ending. It just sort of dwindled away. We saw each other nearly every working day. It didn't hurt to lose her—it just left me with a gnaw of discontent, a feeling of mild guilt and inadequacy. It had all been over for two years, but I could not be at ease with her and I sensed it was the same with her; and always would be. Our bodies were too meaningful to each other. We shared too many lusty memories. The end of love is sadness. This had not been love, but it left a sadness nevertheless.

The desk space I rent is in the rear of the office. I sat at my desk and looked at Sis for a few moments. She sat with her back toward me, typing industriously, sitting very erect in the posture chair. She wore a pale green skirt and a white blouse and sat with her ankles crossed. I looked at the concave curvings where her neat and narrow waist blossomed down to the convexity of her round and solid hips, and I felt that faint visceral shift and stirring of desire for her. I knew it would never be completely dead. But two years had passed and I knew I would never do anything about it. We had been too good together for it to be forgotten. I knew she was dating a lawyer, a widower, but I suspected that if I asked her to come out to the cottage with me, she would look startled, then smile in a remembered, greedy way, and nod her head. But I would not ask her. When something has ended, you can't start it all over from the beginning. It was the beginning of the affair that I missed—that perhaps we both missed—but all we could do would be to start it up once more at the end, and thus end it again.

As I was opening my mail she rolled halfway around on the chair casters and said, "Did they wake you up early with a mess of sirens, Sam?"

"Sirens?"

"I heard it on my car radio this morning. Some old duck is supposed to have spotted that Charlie Haywood down your way at about two in the morning. He reported seeing him in his car lights, ducking back into the brush down near Cass Road. That's not much more than a mile south of you."

"Did they take him seriously?"

"The radio said state and county police are searching the area."

"I think it would be pretty stupid for that fella to head back here, don't you?"

16

"I don't really know, Sam. I guess I'm pulling for him to get away. Does that mean I've got a criminal mind?"

"Probably," I said, and forced a grin. "I got up early because I went to bed early."

"That lousy wind kept waking me up all night. I never sleep right when it's windy. You know Charlie, don't you?"

I shrugged, casually. "I know most of the boys in the automobile agencies in the area. I had a few beers with Charlie Haywood. Pleasant kid, I thought."

"Not a safe-breaker, or safe-cracker or whatever they call them."

"Thief is an easy word."

"Okay, not a thief, Sam."

"But he admitted it."

"I know he did, but that doesn't mean I can't find it hard to believe."

Just then Jennie Benjamin came in, croaking loud greetings. A round, florid woman, she crossed to her desk and banged her straw purse down upon it. She had parlayed a real estate license and a cheerfully abusive personality into a good living by skillfully bullying the indecisive into renting or buying property they did not particularly like. I gave Sis my best guess as to when I would be back. I had two calls to make. I drove up to Venice and checked some rear end damage to a Porsche which had been smacked at a stop sign. The company adjuster had told me the estimate seemed too high, and he had mailed me a photostat of it from Tampa. I got the foreign car parts book out of my wagon and checked the rear bumper segments and bumper guards and the allowable labor costs of replacement. The woman who owned it told me at least four times how come she had been smacked in the rear end at a stop sign. I soon found what had hiked the repair estimate. The left bumper brace had been thrust forward, not only dimpling the shell below the motor compartment, but also bowing a section of the motor compartment upward. It would have to be allowed, but I did find one bumper segment listed for replacement that did not have to be replaced, thus cutting down the repair close to twenty dollars. I told her she would get her check from

Aetna in a few days and she could go ahead now and have her baby fixed up.

I continued on north to Sarasota to check out a toughie. A kid named Hosslar had parked his classic car, a completely restored 1935 Ford Phaeton in the big lot at the South Gate Shopping Center. A semi-senile old foof from Kentucky in all the Chrysler you can buy had hit the gas instead of the brake and lept all his wide span of tailfins backward into the Ford, knocking it sixty feet and rolling it completely over once, right before the eyes of the horrified youngster who was returning to his beauty after making a small purchase.

Technically it was a total loss, and the procedure would have been to pay the kid the appraised value, take over the car in the name of the insurance company and apply any salvage against the loss. But how do you appraise a classic car representing hundreds of hours of painstaking restoration and God knows how many layers of carefully rubbed paint? We went around and around, arguing in the hot sun. I stretched my authority just as far as I could, and it still wasn't fair to the kid, but he finally believed me and trusted me and agreed to it.

It certainly wasn't any total loss to him. It was like a girl friend with a pair of black eyes and a broken arm.

I finished with the kid in time to drive to Anderson Ford and check out a 1960 convertible that had lost an argument with a palm tree. The detailed estimate was two pages long but it was still two hundred bucks under a total loss. I had lunch with Marv Sirus, the sales manager, and we told each other some lies about how well we were bowling lately, and he told me about the Sunday pigeons he plucks on the golf course. I drove back down through Venice to Florence City, debated stopping at the office, but figured it would be best to go right home.

As I slowed to turn into my shell drive, between the two big pepper trees, I wondered if the police, checking the area, had looked my place over. If they had found Charlie there, it might put me in a spot I'd have trouble talking my way out of, but it might work out for the best. If they hadn't found him, I hoped he was willing, ready and able to leave.

Chapter Two

I PARKED by the porch and as I walked toward the door to the living room it opened for me and Charlie Haywood backed away to let me in. He held my .38 revolver in his right hand, aimed down at the floor.

I shut the door and said, "Nice friendly welcome, Charlie."

"I didn't know who was driving up, Sam."

"Somebody you might have to kill, maybe?"

"I don't want to kill anybody. I just want to be left alone until I do what I have to do." He placed the gun carefully on the end table by the couch, half concealed by the big ashtray I keep there.

He looked better. The lumps the insects had left on his face and arms and neck did not look as painful and obvious. My discarded clothing fit him reasonably well. The sneakers were laced tight enough to stay on.

"Want some of your coffee, Sam? I made more than I need."

I sat down with him at the table in the kitchen alcove. "When did you get up?"

"Maybe an hour ago. It was two o'clock by that bedroom clock. I'm sorry, I cooked more of your eggs than I could eat. I thought I could eat everything in the place the way I felt. But I guess my stomach got shrunk."

He took the cigarette I offered with obvious eagerness. "I found the gun when I was hunting around for cigarettes, Sam."

"I didn't think, or I would have left some."

"The ones we get, they're a prison product, you know. Lousy cigarettes. Lousy food. Mostly fatback and beans."

Two years at the camp had toughened this boy. He seemed a lot more calm than I would have been under the circumstances.

"Anybody bother you at all while I was gone?"

"The phone rang once. Eight rings before they gave up. That's all."

"What are your plans, Charlie?"

"Take a nap and then get out of your hair at dusk. Can you drive me into town? Then that will be the end of it."

"You'll be spotted inside one minute, won't you?"

"I found a couple of things you maybe could give me. I could pay you later on, if things work out. I experimented a little." He got up and went into the bedroom. He came out wearing an old baseball hat of mine, with the bill pulled well down. He wore big mirrored sunglasses. And the shape of his face was subtly but so completely changed I would not have recognized him.

"You can have the hat and glasses, but what have you done to your face?"

"Cotton between my lips and my gums, and a couple of wads in my cheeks, Sam. It changes your voice too. I heard about it in that camp. Is it going to work?"

"I think it will, and nobody around here has seen you in over two years."

"Less than that, Sam. Thirteen months. Remember, they let me come to my mother's funeral. With a guard."

"I'd forgotten that."

"I haven't. It's something I add onto the score, Sam. Everything was sold and the money is in an account. When I can come out into the open, I'll pay you for this stuff out of that money."

"Forget it, for God's sake!"

"I don't know what I would have done if you hadn't been willing to help me, Sam. I was right at the end. I didn't have anything left." He picked the cotton out of his mouth, put it in the shirt pocket, took off the hat and glasses and sat down to finish his coffee.

"You were identified at two in the morning a mile or

so south of here. Cass Corners. So the cops are checking the whole area."

He stared at me and then cursed bitterly. "I was so tired I wasn't tracking right. The wind kept me from hearing that car coming and like a damn fool I turned and looked at the lights for a second before I got the hell off the shoulder. It makes it a little rougher, I guess."

"If I knew your plans maybe I could give you some advice."

"Like give up? I don't need anybody else in on this, Sam. I haven't got the right to ask anybody else in on it."

"Somebody told me this morning that she was sure you hadn't done anything criminal. She brought you up because she'd heard the radio report on your being seen in the area."

"Who?"

"Sis Gantry."

"So she got her own name back? I hoped she would."

"She petitioned the court and had it restored."

He looked beyond me, his face softening perceptibly. "I used to run around with two of the Gantry boys that were my age. Billy and Sid. That's how I got to notice Sis. I knew her but I wasn't aware of her until I was, I guess, about fourteen and she was eighteen. And then I got the damnedest crush on her. God, how I hated those big guys who were dating her! When I got within ten feet of her I couldn't breathe and I felt as if I'd faint. If a day went by and I didn't get a chance to look at her and adore her, it was a lost day. I used to imagine the wildest, craziest things about her. Wonderful things, and dirty things too. You know how kids are. She knew how I felt, I guess. She'd kid me a little bit and my face would get so hot it would feel as if it was going to blow up. Sam, you remember Grouper Island?"

"Sure."

"Sis and one of her girlfriends named Louise and another girl whose name I can't remember, they used to sail down there in hot weather in Louise's little sailboat for a picnic and swimming, and then I heard the rumor they went down there to get tan all over, and it nearly drove me out of my mind. I found out the next time they

21

were going and I got down there awful damn early in the morning and landed on the bay side and pulled my little outboard way up into the mangroves and out of sight. By the time they landed on the beach side at noon, I had an observation post that looked right out on the most likely spot.

"The sun was blazing hot, and they established themselves right out in front of me, and before I could get mentally adjusted, they'd spread blankets, stripped themselves right down to the buff and they were rubbing the sun oil on. The first time I saw all there was to see of Sis Gantry, I thought I'd die of love and yearning. She made those other two look like sick, plucked chickens. They kept going into the Gulf to cool off and walking back and stretching out again. I was perfectly hidden, and I wasn't twenty feet from those blankets. By about the third time Sis took a dip, I could stare without feeling dizzy. When they all sat on one blanket, giggling and quacking and splitting up the big picnic lunch, I had time to realize that between hunger and thirst and hungry bugs, I was the most uncomfortable boy in the whole state of Florida.

"By late afternoon when she took her tenth or fifteenth dip in the Gulf, it didn't matter to me whether I looked at her or not. I looked, out of some sense of duty I guess, but a glass of ice water would have looked twice as good and three times as useful. I had no way to sneak out of there. I had to wait it out. And I knew that if they found out about me being there, I'd get half killed.

"When the edge of the sun touched the horizon, those girls sailed away. I never wanted to see another naked woman. They hadn't left a scrap of food or a swallow of coke. I'd spent eleven hours on that island, and the last seven of it on my belly, without food or drink. When I walked back into my house I felt seventy years old and I looked so terrible it scared my mother. I ate so much she stopped worrying.

"The next time I saw Sis in the flesh, I knew my great love had ended somehow. I not only didn't have to wonder what was under her clothes, I kept wishing I could forget. I can still close my eyes and see her padding up the beach toward her blanket. I guess it was about two years later she married that bum."

Charlie Haywood sighed and yawned. "That's a lot of woman going to waste. Is she just the same as ever?"

"If a runaway tiger jumped through the window near her desk, Sis Gantry would scold it for breaking the window, scratch it behind the ear to show she wasn't really mad, then lead it across the street and buy it a steak."

"And she automatically assumes I'm innocent?"

"That's what she said."

He stood up. "I'll wash this stuff up and then go get a nap. You going out again?"

"I'll be back a little after six." I looked at my watch. "It'll be dark enough by seven-thirty to drive you in. Where do you want to be left off?"

"I've decided to give that a little more thought, Sam. I'll know by the time you take me in."

I left him my cigarettes, relocked the cottage, and drove into town and over the bridge to the office next to Orange Beach. Neither Sis nor Jennie Benjamin was there. I knew the boss man wouldn't be in. Tom Earle was taking a summer vacation at a Canadian fishing lodge. Vince Avery was there, in persuasive, low-voiced conversation with a well-padded female prospect. Vince is an incurable lightweight who does everything imaginable to enhance his own fancied resemblance to the Clark Gable of twenty years back.

Alice Jessup came over to my desk as I sat down, and gave me a phone slip to return a Tampa call. She is a sallow, timid girl in her twenties, the only purely clerical and secretarial worker in the office. The associates work on a percentage deal with Tom. Sis has her real estate license and she is half and half. She gets a salary for the secretarial work she does, plus a smaller percentage on those deals she swings.

"Can you fit in a little dictation, Alice?" I asked her.

She blushed, as she invariably does, and said, "Oh, sure, it's real dead around here, believe me. I'll get my book."

Sis and Alice keep a separate account of any time spent on my work and bill me at the end of each month. I dictated the three reports, then returned the Tampa call and learned of two new appraisals to make, one in Osprey and one in Punta Gorda, and I would get the pertinent papers in the morning mail. I walked a half-block south on Orange Road to stand in the murky chill of the Best Beach Bar and nurse a cold dark Loëwenbrau and argue the pennant race with fat, opinionated Gus Herka, owner, proprietor and bartender.

When we had exhausted baseball he said, "Hey, how about that Charlie Haywood? How about him, hey? He was a customer, you know it? Not a steady customer. Just sometimes. Nice looking boy, you know it? Sam, you figure like they say he's come back here, hey, maybe? Why should he do that? Three years to go, more when they catch him. Stupid, you know it?"

"Pretty stupid, Gus," I agreed.

He glared at me. "You know damn well it was stupid, Sam!" That's a thing Gus has. If you agree with him he comes back at you as though you had contradicted him. Sometimes it is difficult for strangers to understand.

Though I was, at the moment, the only customer, he leaned across the bar toward me in a heavily conspiratorial manner. "There's more than meets the eye, you know it?"

"Like what, Gus?"

"Like a week before he got arrested, he come in here late, a little bit drunk, not too bad, lipstick all around his mouth, buys a bottle, you know it? Six dollars. Edgy, he acted. Like he would fight anybody. Not like that boy at all, you know it? He went out with the bottle and drove away. Me, I pulled the blind here to look out like this. See? He had a woman in the car with him, you know it? Saw her under the street light, just the hair on her head, silver as a dime, floozy hair."

"So what does that prove, Gus?"

"You are stupid, Sam, you know it? No broad comes into the case. So a nice boy like that, he has a cheap broad making him edgy and drunk, and she needles him and needles him to come up with big money so he tries something foolish. I seen it a dozen times before, you know it?"

I told him he was a great psychologist, and walked back to the office. The reports were done and on my desk, errorless. Miss Alice Jessup does my work with such speed she cheats herself.

24

I thanked her and sealed the envelopes and said, "It's quarter after five, Alice."

"I know but I got to wait for Sis because she's the one that locks up."

"I'll wait. Where is she?"

"Thanks. She shouldn't be long. It was a rental thing. She went to show the people the house just a little bit before you came in."

I had ten minutes alone in the office before Sis came to a screeching stop out front and trotted in. The white blouse was a bit wilted, the green skirt slightly rumpled. I thought of a fourteen-year-old Charlie watching the beach girls.

"What are you grinning at, Brice?" she demanded.

"A joke I couldn't possibly tell you."

"That kind, eh? Hey, I rented a house."

"Good deal."

"In August any kind of a deal is good." She came and sat on the corner of my desk and looked down at me. "How are you doing, Sam?" she asked, her dark blue eyes solemn.

"I like summers the best, and this is a good one. Fishing, swimming, reading, and not too much work. A little bowling, with beer to top it off."

"Have you got a girl these days, Sam?"

"No girl."

"Maybe that isn't even healthy, dear."

"Maybe it isn't. But it's sure peaceful."

"Was I such a nuisance—way back when I was your girl?"

"You were just right, Sis, in every way."

As she looked at me I saw a little bit of the hurt she had so honorably concealed from me for so long. "If I was right, Sam. And what we had was certainly right ..."

"Then I'm the wrong one. Not right for you, or for anybody."

"And I know what's wrong with you, Sam. It took me a long time. But now I know what it is."

"The brand Judy left on me?"

"You enjoy bleeding over that goddam Judy, don't you? Not that, Sam. No. It's something basic in you. You've never decided what you are, Sam. You want to be all meat and muscle and reflexes. You want to deny how bright and intuitive and sensitive you are. You're a complex animal, Sam. You try not to think, and so you think too much. You couldn't just plain love, Sam. You thought us to death. You like to talk ignorant and act ignorant. It's some kind of crazy protective coloration. Maybe you think it's manly. I don't know. You seem to have to . . . diminish yourself. But people sense that good mind, and it makes them uncomfortable because you are being something you're not."

"Standard pattern," I said, and faked a yawn. "You overcomplicate it. I'm a simple guy, with simple needs."

"Oh sure. That guard certainly comes up fast when anybody tries to get too close to you. Anyway, what I want to tell you is I think I might get married."

"To that lawyer?"

"Yes. To Cal McAllen."

"Love him?"

"I like him. I respect him. Maybe that question is academic. I loved Pritch like crazy. I'm twenty-nine, Sam, and I was built for babies, as any fool can plainly see, and time is beginning to run out. He's forty-four, and wise and steady and loving, and he makes me feel completely girlish."

"A for Amour. B for Bed. How is the bed part?"

"Always fundamental, aren't you, Brice? There's been none. I don't know how it will be. This is a very conventional guy, and he is protecting me from his base desires so I can be a girl-type bride. I think I know what I'm getting into, Sam. The male-female thing isn't something I'd have to look up in the World Book Encyclopedia, exactly. He'll always miss his first wife a little, and I won't resent that. I get along fine with those two college kids of his. Should I do it, Sam? Should I try to make it work? I want babies, as fast as I can have them."

"And you're asking me?"

"Because you know me. And because I trust you."

"I don't want you to think I'm being coarse or trivial when I tell you how I think, Sis."

"You have your own kind of sense. You can say anything to me, Sam. You know that." She giggled. "Come

26

to think of it, I guess you've said everything to me there is to say."

"Hush a minute. You are a very lusty, vital, hot-blooded, demanding wench."

"Oh, thank you, sir!"

"You are going to be, to put it mildly, a sexual responsibility to this guy if you marry him."

"So?"

"So, as of now, you don't love him. But if he can . . . discharge the responsibilities of his office and set you up in the motherhood department, and if you like him already, you are going to end up loving him and it is going to be fine."

"If, if. You keep saying *if*."

"But if the bed part is bad, the whole thing is going to be a trap you'll be too stubborn to try to get out of, and it will be a hell on earth, because the physical part of it is going to be a lot more essential a part of marriage to you than it might be to a lot of other women."

"I can see it coming, you scoundrel. I should seduce the gentleman."

"It makes sense, Sis."

"My little schemes have failed thus far. Got any ideas?"

"Have you told him yes yet?"

"No."

"Then do so, and drive to some motel outside the county and celebrate the coming marriage, and if it doesn't work out, change your mind."

"And hurt him?"

"If it doesn't work out, you won't be squeamish about hurting him."

She beamed and said, "Maybe you are a wise man."

"I can only be wise about other people. Take care, Sis."

I reached the door and put my hand on the latch and then turned and frowned at her and said, "There's one other thing that should be done."

"Yes?"

"But it might not be too smart. Skip it."

She came quickly to me and hooked two fingers in my shirt pocket and gave an irritable tug and said, "What, Sam? What other thing?"

27

"Well, it sort of relates to the fact that knowledge is power."

She stamped her foot. "Stop being so damn shifty!"

"I just had the idea that before you get this motel deal all set up, you could send Cal to me for detailed information on the best way to attack this special problem he'll be facing . . . uh . . . what to do and what not to do . . ."

She tried a hard right and I caught that wrist, and I just barely caught the left wrist in time to jump out of the way of some very sincere kicks. Her face was bright red and she was grunting with effort and trying to keep from laughing at the same time.

"Oh, you dirty stinking thing!" she groaned.

When I felt the tension go out of her muscles I cautiously released her. We were standing close, and smiling at each other.

"You are a monster," she said gently.

"I bet you can lick that lawyer man in a fair fight, lady."

Her breasts lifted and fell with a mighty sigh as she looked up at me, and I saw the way her eyes and her mouth changed.

"Sam, my darling, you'll always be a part of my life," she whispered.

"It was a good part, wasn't it?"

She dropped her eyes and said, "This is . . . shameless and disloyal and . . . and sick, I guess. But could we . . . what was that word you used? . . . celebrate once more what it all used to be? Sam?"

Right at the edge of an eager agreement, no matter how unwise, I remembered Charlie. "Could you . . . drive out about nine o'clock, or could I pick you up?"

She took another deep shuddering breath and then squared her shoulders and said, "No, dear. That would be too cold-blooded, and it would give me too much time to think and . . . too much guilt afterward. If it could have happened right now . . . if you could have broken speed laws taking me down to the cottage . . . The hell with it, Sam. At very best it was a very bad idea."

"I hope you'll be happy, Sis."

"I want enough of them so I can name one of them Sam without anybody getting any cute ideas about it."

"If they're all girls?"

"Sam is still a good name."

As I walked by the front of the building toward my car I looked in and saw her covering her typewriter, her face thoughtful. She looked up and smiled and gave me a final bawdy wink.

After I had crawled into the bread-baking heat of the wagon I remembered too late, the tailored red leather couch in Tom Earle's small private office. She was right —I was a monster, a hopeless lecher. It made me feel guilty to realize it had even entered my mind. I knew Sis well enough to know she would have taken the offer of the random bounce on her employer's red couch in one of two ways. She would have become savagely angry or semi-hysterical with laughter. With all her potential of eagerness, she yet required that dignity which is a product of total privacy and ample time.

As I drove over toward town to check a claim that could be looked at only after working hours, I improved my morale by telling myself no hopeless lecher could long endure without a girl. And I was enduring quite well, and was convinced that the months of girllessness were not corroding my masculinity in any way. And how many months was it? Five and a bit, since that turbulent weekend in March with that miraculous tourist lady down in Fort Myers. A policy holder with one of my client companies had stove in the front of her husband's blue Buick and, for business reasons, he had to fly back to Philadelphia, leaving her to wait for the repairs and then drive the car north. I came onto the scene after the husband had departed, and she had described him for me, saying, "This is the first time in our entire married life that I have had one minute of freedom from that tubby, arrogant, possessive, jealous little man, and I certainly do not intend to spend the rest of my life daydreaming wistfully what I might have done the only damned time I was ever given a chance, Mr. Brice. So might we carry these drinks into the bedroom?"

She had been a tall carroty redhead, so uncompromisingly scrawny that I would have never considered making

29

a pass at her. But her approach had been so shockingly abrupt, I couldn't think of any simple way to evade it, and there didn't seem to be time for any complicated way. So I found myself, drink in hand, trailing her stupidly into the bedroom of the motel suite. I soon found that the look of scrawniness disappeared completely when the clothing was gone. I was the instrument by which she was determined to avenge herself on life for dealing her sixteen years of very dreary marriage, and she was almost frighteningly determined not to waste a single moment. I went to look at the Buick on Friday afternoon and finally got to look at it on Monday morning, and I had to work fifteen straight twelve-hour days to catch up on my work after that redheaded weekend.

Aside from such unexpected, unsought interludes, I was learning that a man can live without a woman. Sometimes the house is too empty. Sometimes the restlessness is like sickness. But I guess I wasn't learning to live without any woman. I was still learning to live without Judy.

I met Judy Caldwell during the tail end of the season of my last year of college ball. I was two months away from twenty-two, and she was a nineteen-year-old import from a girls' college in the east, flown in for the football weekend by a fraternity brother who was so serious about her and had talked so much about her that we were prepared for a letdown. But when Judy entered a room and when she smiled and looked around, before saying a word, she turned all other females in the room to wax and ashes. With that careful, casual ruff of blonde amorous hair, the mobile mouth, those bottomless violet eyes, and her trim, taut look of tension under control, I thought her the most alive thing I had ever seen in my life. Before I ever heard her voice, I wanted to own her forever.

She was, in the most comprehensive meaning of the phrase, a status symbol. In any given year there are not many nineteen-year-old girls of that wondrous breed. In a generation there are pitifully few—in any age bracket.

If you acquire one of them, you can walk them into any public place in the civilized world and be marked at once as a man of rare luck, and special talent.

Some of them move inevitably into the entertainment

world. Liz Taylor and Julie Newmar are in that special pattern.

They are beautiful and animated and they live deeply, wildly, constantly on some far out edge of emotional tension. They are incomparably feminine. They need and seek all the symbols of male strength, despising weak men. When they have decided exactly what they want, they go after it with a ruthlessness that would confound any pirate. No one can predict their next mood, especially themselves.

They are tidy as panthers, and as blandly vain. Physically, they are like a blow at the heart. The skin texture is so flawless as to be unreal. Their bodies, in repose, or in movement, have an intricacy of curvings, lines, textures and hollows that make other women look curiously unfinished. They eat like wolves, laugh with the throat open wide, and wear the face of a child when they sleep. They sense that they are placed here for the purpose of living—and there will never be enough time for all of it.

In any ten-minute span they can take you through fifty emotions, which will include a great many you never heard of and can never describe.

In the bleakness of the jealousy of the men who cannot have them and the women who cannot match them, petty words are spoken: shallow, silly, arrogant, spoiled, wild, untrustworthy . . .

But to the few men in each generation who can possess one of these, to the extent that any of them can be truly possessed, they are the incomparable reward. They love with a savage, surpassing joy. They have passion without limit. They are so far beyond any restraint that it becomes a special innocence, touching and beyond price.

Judy was one of that unique sisterhood and she was, of course, a status symbol. And she could not avoid or prevent those things that weigh so heavily on the other end of the scale.

You find yourself so unashamedly adored that the bright hot light of that adoration constantly illuminates your own unworthiness.

And the status symbol works both ways. You must be her symbol also. Defeat is unforgivable, because she equates defeat with weakness. She who is destined to belong to kings can never scrub cottages. She goes with success, and she leaves with it also.

And once you have been showered by that special bounty, you can never fit yourself comfortably back into that world from which all magic has fled. She is in your nerves and your blood and your flesh forever.

All you can do is try to avoid comparison, because it can be a knife in your heart. I kept her out of my mind when I was with Sis. But there was one time when she slipped past my defenses, and suddenly I was in the midst of a coarse, meaningless, doughy frolic with some strange dull girl, and it all stopped within a single heavy beat of my heart. I had to plead a sudden illness—wondering aloud about food poisoning, knowing I could not speak of the poisoned heart. I went alone into the night and stood on my dock and looked at the stars and told all the smiling ghosts of Judy that it wasn't fair to take everything away. She must have relented, because it was once more the way it should be with Sis when we were together again.

I checked the freshly battered junker in town, and so it was a little after seven on that August evening when I got back to the cottage. Charlie had just finished off a fried slab of the morning snook. He said he had slept until six, when the alarm had awakened him. He did not think the phone had rung again, or that anybody had knocked at my door. He said he was ready to go as soon as it was dark enough.

"You certainly seem calm, Charlie."

"When you know what you're going to do, there's no point in worrying any more. You can start worrying again if it doesn't work."

"About the gun, I hope you're not going to ask me if you can please borrow the gun."

"I won't need a gun. Sam, are you trying to find out what I'm going to do?"

"I don't think I want to know what you're going to do. I have the feeling that already I know more than I want to know. You were picked up when you were working on the safe out at the Weber house on the Key. You got pretty bitter about Charity Weber. I can think of all kinds of things that could have been going on,

32

and I don't want any more clues."

He opened a fresh pack of cigarettes I had brought him and said, "I guess you don't want to get mixed up in anything, Sam."

"What do you mean?"

He shrugged. "You got it the way you want it, I guess. There's nothing wrong with it. It's like you got a hole and you pulled it in after you. That's another reason I came here. I knew you'd live quiet and keep your head down. I guessed you wouldn't turn me in, and I guessed you wouldn't try to help me, either. I don't want any help. I can tell right now how anxious you are to be rid of me, so you can forget you had anything to do with it."

"It sounds as if you—"

"I'm not criticizing you, Sam. It's your life and your choice, and maybe a hell of a lot of people would be better off if they just stepped aside the way you have. You've got the books and the records and that little boat tied up to your dock down there, and a job that doesn't get you too involved. I guess I envy you."

He stepped over to the sink and began to scrub the frying pan.

"I'll do that later on, Charlie."

"No trouble. That's a damn fine fish."

"I can let you have twenty bucks to take along with you if it would help out."

"Thanks, Sam. It'll help. Even if I find out I don't need it, it will help the morale to have it in my pocket."

We left the cottage at twenty minutes of eight. During the four-mile trip to the city line the neon gets more frequent and more expensive. He crouched on the floor beside me, one shoulder tucked down under the glove compartment. He had asked to be let off in town handy to some pay phone he could use with a minimum chance of being seen and recognized. I had suggested the outdoor booth at West Plaza, at the big shopping section, not far from the mainland end of City Bridge. The booth was brightly lighted, but set so deep in the parking area, so far from traffic that it was unlikely anyone would come within a hundred feet of him.

Charlie said it sounded all right. I pulled off into the shadows of the lot, away from the street lights. The stores were closed, their night lights shining. The big drugstore was open, with fifteen or twenty parked cars clustered close to it. All the rest was a dark desert of empty asphalt. He moved up onto the seat, poked the cotton into place, tugged the bill of the cap down to eyebrow level. The sunglasses were in the breast pocket of the sports shirt, along with the cigarettes I had brought him. "Thanks a lot, Sam," he said.

We shook hands. His hand was hot and dry, leathery with callouses. "Best of luck, Charlie."

He got out of the wagon and walked toward the booth. I could see nothing furtive about the way he walked. He did not look back. I saw him step into the booth, close the folding door and open the phone book. I swung around in a big arc and headed out onto the street.

I could have gone home. That was what I wanted to do. I wanted to cook myself a meal, put the sheets and pajamas he had used in the laundry bundle, clean the place up, put Peggy Lee on the changer and go sit on my screened porch in the dark, in the canvas womb of the safari chair, and drink some big drinks and think small, random, unimportant thoughts, and listen to Peggy and forget the existence of Charlie Haywood. Sis was to be married. Judy was forever lost to me. Charlie would never bring me into his problems again.

I will never know why I didn't do just that.

It's what I should have done.

But there was something particularly touching about the gallantry of the new Charlie Haywood. He had been an ineffectual boy. They had ground him into a man. Maybe I wanted to help him. Or maybe I just wanted to watch. Maybe he had stung me a little with his remarks about having crawled into a hole and pulled it in after me. I knew how true it was. I knew why I had done it. But it hurt my pride to have it pointed out. The big wheel had gone too fast for me, and it had flung me off, and I wasn't about to climb back on.

So instead of heading on home, I hit the brake at the first cross street and doubled all the way back and came back onto the parking lot from the far side.

It wouldn't hurt me at all, I told myself, to kill another ten minutes and see what Charlie did next.

Chapter Three

I PARKED on the far side of the group of cars near the drugstore. I slid out and stood up cautiously and looked out across the roofs of the cars toward the distant booth. He was still in there, and he was talking over the phone. I saw him hang up and step out of the booth. He walked a dozen feet, paused in a hesitant way, and then came angling over toward the drugstore, giving a perfect imitation of a man killing time. I could guess at what the casual manner was costing him.

I pleaded with him mentally not to go into the drugstore. There was a gift shop beside the drugstore. The night lights were on in the gift shop. The show window was illuminated, but not brilliantly. He stopped there and stood with his hands in his pockets, looking at the merchandise.

It was a perfect device. He was just outside the brightness that streamed out of the drugstore, yet he looked as if he might be waiting for someone to come out.

I had gotten back behind the wheel. I could see him through the windows of the car next to mine, a spare shadowy figure in the humid night.

Now what? I asked myself. Sam Brice, public eye. On any T.V. show they would have cast me as the heavy. Maybe at twenty-nine, moving too fast toward thirty, I would still have been acceptable for the rugged hero part had I not spent eleven seasons in football. Four in junior high and Florence City High, as All-State fullback. Four in the semi-pro brand of college ball played in Georgia, as defensive linebacker and defensive end. Three seasons—almost three seasons—in the National Football

35

League as a 215-pound offensive tackle, a little bit light for that job of work, but compensating with quickness and balance.

Take those eleven years of eating cleats and spitting blood and being bounced off the frozen turf, and add the unavoidable social fist fights, and you have a face to loan bill collectors. Store teeth, a crooked jaw, a potato nose, miscellaneous scars and lumps and the tracery of long ago clamps and stitches.

It is, as they keep saying, a sport involving body contact. If I was casting the T.V. series, I would put myself in as the big dumb ugly assistant to the brilliant hero, the comedy relief who bungles the simplest orders, but comes through with the muscle in the clutch. The weight is still at 215, but it requires work and thought to keep it there, and I often wonder why I bother. An automatic reflex in the pride department, perhaps.

The long minutes went by. Kids came out of the drugstore and drove away. Replacements arrived.

Finally a curious thing happened. The stodgy little black Renault turned in and went chugging across the great expanse of empty parking area. It gave one irritable bleat of the horn. Charlie was already on his way toward it. It had stopped thirty feet from the phone booth.

I didn't begin to actually believe it until he had gotten into the little car and it had started up again. She had bought it way back when we had been together. She had driven out to the cottage with it many many times.

I wanted to know what right Charlie had to bring Sis Gantry into the picture. I didn't have to ask myself why she'd let herself be sucked in. Anything with a broken wing would get her immediate attention.

Suddenly I knew it was my fault. I had told Charlie of her blind belief in his innocence. He had needed someone for some service I either couldn't handle, or he had decided I wouldn't handle. He had been sorting over the people he knew, wondering who to ask. And I had handed him Sis on a platter.

"Goddam you, Charlie Haywood," I muttered, and swung around into amateur pursuit. The streets of Florence City are too empty on any given night in August.

I knew Charlie would be alert for any sign of a car following them. And I knew both of them would know my wagon, Sis particularly.

It helped a great deal to have them head directly for the causeway and City Bridge. Horseshoe Key is five miles long and in all its length it is seldom over a quarter-mile wide. Orange Road is the paved road that extends the full length of the Key. The commercial strip takes up most of a mile, right in the middle of the Key opposite the bridge and including the Orange Beach section. If you turn right when you get onto the Key, you head north through the junkier part of the commercial section, and then through an area of cottages and beach houses set too close together, until the road ends at the North Pass Public Beach. If you turn south you pass stores, bars, restaurants, and then a batch of pretentious motels with pretentious names, and suddenly you are in the land of the Large Money, the big homes you can't see from the road, and you can read all the neat signs that say No Stopping, No Trespassing, No Deep Breathing. There is a barricade and a turnaround at the end. In the summer you can risk parking there and walking out along a narrowing sandspit to a good place to cast out into Horseshoe Pass after mackerel and blues. But if you try it in the winter season, you can find your car expensively ticketed.

I hung well back and didn't speed up until I saw the Renault turn left. When I made the turn the road was empty. No small ruby taillights. The road was straight for so far, I knew they had ducked off, and I would have had a lot of trouble learning where—had I not seen too much light coming out of Tom Earle's office.

I slowed down and as I went by, saw the two of them walking from the front door back toward Tom's private office. Evidently they had just walked in and she had clicked on the additional light a moment before I saw it. The Renault was tucked close to the side of the building, its lights out. I used a motel drive for a u-turn and when I went by again I could see neither of them. I turned into the small parking area next to the Best Beach Bar, cut the lights and motor and wondered what the hell to

37

do next. It had ceased being any of my business, and I should have gone home. If Sis got into any trouble, it would be Cal McAllen's problem, not mine. I could think of no reason in the world for her to have taken Charlie right to the office. It bothered me.

I got out and rubbed a thumbnail along the evening bristle on my jaw. I yearned for my dark porch, a tall drink, and the special timing of Miss Lee.

But I kept remembering Tom's office has two windows on the rear of the building. So I went back there, stepping on something that broke with a sharp snapping sound, then kicking an empty can a dozen feet—about as stealthy as a drunken actor falling into the drums. An unseen cat spoke irritably to me. A mosquito did slow rolls inside my ear.

The blinds were down, the slats closed, but like most Venetian blinds the closure was less than perfect. From the first window I could see a section of the closed door and a segment of red leather couch and an edge of one of Tom's framed pictures of himself receiving an award of some kind for civic virtue. The other window was better. I could see part of the shoulder of the sport shirt I had given Charlie, and I had a closeup of the back of his ear, so close that I was startled into backing away. I looked again, over his shoulder, and I saw a slice of Sis's face. She was sitting at the desk, talking into Tom's red telephone. He has a fixation about red, from T'Bird and speedboat to his wife's gaudy hair. But the reds he surrounds himself with make her look like gray carroty death.

The windows were sealed shut. I could see the movement of her lips, but I could hear no sound. Charlie moved out of my range of vision and reappeared beside Sis, bending to whisper into her ear as she momentarily covered the mouthpiece.

Many things dropped neatly into place all of a sudden. Charlie had been happy to sacrifice his freedom as some unknown service to Charity Weber. He had changed his mind in prison. He had to get hold of Charity. She would be the one who could clear him. He couldn't risk phoning her. Sis could make the call and perhaps decoy

Charity Weber into a situation where Charlie could get to her and talk to her. Once it was set up, he would have no more need for Sis's services. Suddenly I remembered how very calm Charlie had seemed after he had gotten some rest. It wasn't a very healthy calm. Suppose he was using Sis to decoy the woman into a situation where he could kill her. With his hands. He hadn't wanted the gun. That would be nice. That would be very nice for everybody.

So it wouldn't hurt to follow the whole deal a little longer.

I wanted to be in the car, ready to go. I started back toward my car. I had to pass once again behind the big new furniture store between the Best Beach Bar and the office.

After I had gone forty feet the flashlight beam struck me in the face. It was about ten feet away. It had nice new batteries in it. Surprises make me irritable. And I strongly disapprove of bright lights glaring into my eyes.

I wrenched my head around and said, "Cut it out!"

"Who you and what you doin' back here?"

Because I was born and raised in Florida, I have often been accused of 'mush-mouf' diction, even though it seems to me I talk the same as anyone else. But this was basic swamp-talk I was hearing, the back country, slough and 'gator, grits and pellagra whine, full of a mock servility, yet flavored with an arrogance born of self knowledge of a special toughness that must be constantly tested to make certain it is still undiluted. I should have recited my name, address and occupation like an obedient child, and told him I had come back to check the rear door of the office building because I had wondered whether I had left it unlocked.

But he kept the light on my face, so I said, "I'm gathering mushrooms." I took a step toward him and said, "Now get out of my way."

The light went off. I had half a second in which to wonder if I was handling this very well, and then I had the same sensation as if a cherry bomb had been firmly taped to my skull over the left ear and detonated. The whole world jumped eight inches eastward. I felt the jar as I went down onto my knees, and I listened to a roaring that went fading, echoing, down through spiral staircases in the back of my brain.

The light was on me again and he said, in a tone of warm appreciation: "Well, you one tough son of a bitch! Plenty big, anyways."

He moved to the side and I heard a faint whisper. The second bomb cracked a crater near the crown of my head and I spread myself gently, face down, into the warm and placid Gulf, floating, while all the girls were laughing and Miss Lee sang. I felt him wrench my arms around behind me, felt a meaningless coolness of metal on my wrists. I felt him pry my wallet out of my hip pocket.

I rested. I was very tired.

He kicked me in the ribs, with insistence rather than brutality. "On your feet, boy. Pick all youself up an stand tall for LeRoy."

I made the first effort and he gave me some help. When I was on my feet I felt tall and frail and a little bit sick to my stomach. He walked behind me, and gave me little jabs in the kidneys with the night stick to steer me in the proper direction. I got into the front seat of the dark blue sedan with the county decal on the door. I had to sit on the edge of the seat.

As he started up I realized I was once again capable of speech. "You're making a mistake," I said humbly.

"Now don't we all, sooner or later."

I had the feeling LeRoy and I were never going to strike up much of a friendship. He headed across the bridge to the mainland, driving without haste.

"You a new deputy?" I asked him.

"Best part of a year. You got a name?"

"Samuel Collins Brice."

"Then you didn't steal the money wallet maybe?"

"No, I didn't steal the money wallet maybe."

I got my first good look at him in the bridge lights. The brim of his ranch hat shadowed a pinched and narrow little face. His neck was too scrawny for the collar of the khaki shirt. He was about the size of a fourteen year old who had been sick and underfed. He kept his chin high in order to see over the hood, and he held the wheel firmly in his little brown hands.

"And what is your name, Mister Deputy, sir?"

"Depity LeRoy Luxey."

"I've seen your name in the paper a lot lately. You make a lot of arrests."

"If a man is put hisself in the arrestin' trade, and does his work good, it comes out thataway somehow."

He drove through empty streets and through the open iron gate into the courtyard area behind the Florence County Courthouse. Golden light shone through an open door onto the old brick paving, and as he herded me out of the car, I heard some men laughing. I didn't know whether to be relieved or depressed to identify the rumbling bark of Sheriff Pat Millhaus.

As you go through the door you enter a corridor which has been narrowed by the addition of a waist-high counter on your right. Pat Millhaus lounged behind the counter with an inch of dead cigar in the corner of his mouth, a blue sports shirt—sweat-dark at the armpits—strained across the mound of hard belly. He was talking across the counter to a man I did not know, an old gentleman in a white linen suit that had turned to an ivory yellow with age.

Pat stared at me, his little dark eyes opening very round and wide, and suddenly they were squeezed into slits in the dark hard flesh of his face as he began to laugh. He laughed a lot longer than was necessary.

When he paused for breath, LeRoy Luxey asked gently, "You'd maybe be laughin' at me, Sher'f?"

There was, implicit in that mild question, a terrible and innocent ferocity. Pat had half-tamed a wild thing and was using it for his own purposes. But it had to be handled with extraordinary care. I sensed, and so did Pat Millhaus, that if he had answered yes, the stringy little man would have immediately begun the blind and automatic and inescapable process of trying to kill his superior officer. The structure of his pride would have permitted no alternative.

The sheriff sobered at once and said, "I'm laughing at this damn fool you brung in, LeRoy. I've known him . . .

just about eleven years. What's the story on him, LeRoy."

"I was checking the beach like you said on account of the B and E that's been a-goin' on out there, and I come on this Brice sneakin' along behind of the Gulfway Furniture. I put the light on him and ast him what's he doing, and he makes me some smart-mouth talk and comes at me, so I thumped him some and brang him on in. This here is the money wallet I took off'n him, and he's got no knife or gun, Sher'f."

"He talked smart, LeRoy, because he keeps forgetting somehow he isn't a big time operator with his name in the papers any more. What were you doing out there, Sam?"

"I had the feeling I'd left the back door at Tom Earle's office unlocked. I parked my car at Gus Herka's place and walked back to check it. I was going back to Gus's to get a beer and then go home when I was stopped by . . . your eager little assistant."

"Would you be stupid enough to get any fancy ideas about lawing LeRoy here for assault and false arrest?"

"I think I asked for what I got, Pat."

"We'll get your name on a release form before you go, just in case. Unloose him there, LeRoy."

When my hands were free, I fingered the damage. The one over the ear had left a knot the size of half a plum. It had creased the skin slightly, but the blood had caked in my hair. The other was smaller.

"If you can give me that release form," I said.

"I think we ought to set and talk some," Pat said. "We've never had a chance to talk since you come back to town, you know that?"

"I've never had the urge," I told him. "I don't have it now."

"I could whip his haid a little more so's he'd talk polite," LeRoy said earnestly.

"I think you better get back on duty, LeRoy," Pat Millhaus said. "This man has no record—at least not down here. He just has the habit of thinking he's a little bit better than anybody else."

The old gentleman, after staring at me with open curiosity, said good night to Pat and left. Pat took me down a corridor past his radio communications center to his office. He directed me to a straight chair in the middle of the room, facing his desk. He went behind his desk and lowered himself into a big green leather chair and stared at me with bland satisfaction. Except for black hair cropped so short the brown skull shows through, he looks like one of those old prints of the fat Indian chiefs who got annoyed with Custer.

Pat Millhaus is a good politician and a reasonably adequate law officer.

He played football for Florida Western. While I was playing for Florence City High he was a deputy sheriff who, by a rearrangement of his duty schedule, was able to work with the Florence City High coaching staff on a volunteer basis. It took me a long time to figure out why he singled me out. I finally realized it was because of all the members of the squad, I was the one who was obviously better than he had ever been. He rode me hard throughout those two seasons. The last game of my senior year was a night game. We won. After I had showered and changed, Millhaus and I went out back of the gym, all alone in the bright white moonlight. I was nineteen and I weighed one ninety. He was twenty-six and weighed two twenty. I had more height and reach, but I had played three quarters of a hard game that same night.

We fought for over an hour. We beat each other to bloody ruin. At times I couldn't remember who I was fighting or why. At times we rested, our lungs creaking, our arms like dead meat, and then went at it again. I don't know how many times I got up from the cool moist grass, back onto my feet, when I thought I'd never make it. I don't know how many times I watched him climbing ponderously, slowly back onto his feet, as I waited, praying he wouldn't make it.

It was a standoff. Afterwards we required medical and surgical attention and bed rest. Neither of us was worth a damn for a couple of weeks.

Folklore says that such an experience creates undying friendship. But it neither enhanced or reduced our hatred.

"It's a shameful thing to come so far down in the world

you've got fellas like LeRoy putting knots on your All-American skull, Sam."

"He's a little quick with that stick."

"It's a shame you can't call a press conference."

"Knock it off, Millhaus."

He shook his big head sadly. "There you were, right on top of the heap. Finest tackle in the league they were calling you. Had what they call a shining future. Had that blonde wife that could make a fella go all sweaty just seeing her half a block away."

"You've been waiting for this a long time, Pat. So have your fun."

"But you were always so much more important than anybody else you figured you could make your own rules. So you got real cute, and you got thrown out of pro football for life. Oh, I know it didn't get into the papers because that was part of the agreement. The papers talked about a bad knee you didn't have. But they had to unload you, Brice, because they couldn't take a chance on you throwing a ball game for a little cash money."

"Enjoy yourself."

"And when all of a sudden they busted you right down to nothing, you didn't have a thing left to sorta hold the interest of that fancy little wife. Guess she decided if you were going to live under a cloud, you could live there all by yourself."

"You're a son of a bitch."

He smiled comfortably. "I'm a sheriff son of a bitch, Sam. You're a crooked ballplayer son of a bitch. And I'd love for you to get into some real trouble around here sometime, so you could see how I operate this department. And if you felt you were being treated less than fair, who would you yell to? Since that last uncle died, you've got no kin down here. No special friends. People figure you think you're too good for the common folk. You're a loner, Sam." He leaned forward, "And there isn't one soul in the big world gives enough of a damn about you to care what the hell I might do to you, given half a chance."

"I'm intrigued to see how you can use your position to lean on me, Pat, instead of trying to pick up Charlie.

I saw the flicker of a dangerous anger in his dark eyes. It went away as he leaned back in his big chair. "Right dangerous character, that Charlie Haywood."

"Who knows?"

"He's off in the brush someplace being et up by bugs. When he gets hungry enough and discouraged enough, he'll come on out like a lamb. To save you from sitting here worrying about my business, I better let you sign the release and go on about your business."

He filled in the blanks in a standard release and I signed it and two of his people witnessed it. I had been apprehended and brought it voluntarily for questioning and released with no charges placed against me.

"How do I get back to my car?"

"A man who made all the money you made just for knocking folks down should be able to figure something out."

I walked three blocks to the bus station where I phoned a cab which took me over to my car. I had recurrent waves of nausea which effectively canceled any idea of the dinner I hadn't had yet. I drove back to the cottage and showered and went straight to bed. In spite of a thumping headache, I went to sleep in minutes. But I kept waking myself up during the night by rolling onto my left side and putting too much pressure on the knot over my ear.

Chapter Four

WHEN I PARKED by the office at twenty after nine the next morning, Jennie Benjamin, Alice Jessup and Vince Avery were standing in the morning shade of the building looking irritable.

"I've heard the phone ringing in there," Alice said. "What will people think?"

"You do have a key, old man?" Vince said hopefully. "I've mislaid mine. Jennie's is home, and Alice was never given one."

"Sis hasn't showed up?" I asked as I walked toward the door, sorting out the right key.

"A flaw in her alarming efficiency," Vince said. "And damned inconvenient."

"I phoned from across the street," Alice said, "but she isn't home."

After I let them in I went across the street and had an enormous breakfast. I had thought the major lump too diminished to be noticeable, but old Cy said, "One of your women club you, Sambo?"

"Just a love tap."

"If that's love, don't you never rile that woman. You single fellers lead a right interesting life."

"We're busy every minute. I keep a supply penned up out behind the place, Cy. Every evening I go out there, make a choice, then I turn her loose in the morning."

"Don't that upset the neighbors some?"

"Only when they all get to baying at the same time, those nights the moon is full. It gets hard to hear yourself think out there."

46

As he refilled my coffee cup, he said, "What you should have done, Samuel, was tie up that Sis Gantry permanent when you had the chance."

"Everybody gives me advice."

"I'm sixty-four years old and I don't look a day over seventy, but I got an eye for that young stuff, and I watched her enough so I got me the idea she'd do you better than that whole pen full of women you got out there, baying and all. Might even be she'd need a whole pen full of fellers like you."

"You run a clean food operation, Cy, but you've got a dirty mind."

"A man talks about the ways of nature these days and somehow it gets to be called dirt. Honest to God, Sam, how did you get that chunk on the head?"

"I had a little misunderstanding with a deputy I'd never met before."

"LeRoy Luxey, I bet a dollar."

"No bet, Cy."

"He's mean and edgy as a cottonmouth, that one. They had to get him out of Collier County this spring before he killed off some folks down there that couldn't get to like him. His daddy has some political push, so he got saddled onto Pat Millhaus. Was it last night?"

"Yes."

"It isn't many people you find walking around eating a big breakfast the morning after they get into a little discussion with that Luxey."

"My brain pan is located next to the stomach, Cy. The head is solid bone all the way through. It's a requirement for all professional athletes."

I walked back to the pay phone beyond the magazine racks and called the Gantry house on Jackson Street. Joe and Lois Gantry still live in the big old frame house that used to belong to Lois's people. Joe has worked for the phone company all his life and he is nearing retirement age. Of the nine kids, six of the boys are married—with only two of the married ones still living in the area. The youngest boy is still in high school and lives at home. The next to the youngest is in Florida State, and working on a shrimp boat out of Tampa summers.

Mrs. Gantry answered the phone and when I told her who it was, she said, "Oh." She put a world of meaning into that single flat monosyllable. She had guessed the relationship I had enjoyed with her widowed daughter, and she had resented it and cherished the hope it would blossom into marriage, and had blamed me when we broke up.

"Sis hasn't showed up here yet, Mrs. Gantry." I listened to a silence that promised to continue indefinitely. "Is she home?"

"No, Mr. Brice."

"Well . . . do you know where she is?"

Her worry overwhelmed her strong feelings about me. "No, I don't, and I wish I did. She didn't come home all night. She got a phone call last night a little before eight o'clock and she went out without saying who phoned her, and she just . . . hasn't come back. I phoned Mr. McAllen but he hasn't seen her. And I . . . phoned your place a little while ago but there was no answer." I knew what it had cost her to make that call, and to tell me she had made it.

"She didn't pack a bag or anything, as if she was going on a trip?"

"Oh, no! She didn't do anything like that. She practically didn't change a thing to go out, so I knew it wasn't very important. We were watching television when she got the call. She kept on the same dark red halter top and just changed from shorts to some gray slacks and put on some sandals and . . . said she'd see us later. I didn't even know she hadn't come home until I looked into her room this morning. I keep wondering whether to tell the police."

"Maybe it would be a good idea, Mrs. Gantry."

"Are you hinting about something you're not telling me?"

"No. She's a reliable gal. It isn't like her to go off on impulse, is it?"

"No, it isn't . . ."

"And she would have phoned so you wouldn't be worried."

"Yes, I guess she . . ."

"If she should phone the office or if I learn anything, I'll let you know right away, Mrs. Gantry."

"Thanks, Mr. Br . . . Sam."

After I took care of twenty minutes of desk work, I drove to Boca Grande and made it in a little less than fifty minutes. An insured from New Jersey had clipped a column and brought a large chunk of the roof of an old hotel garage down onto the top of his Chrysler Imperial. I had made an appointment with a local builder to meet me at the scene, and we went over his estimate with the owner. The column was powdery with dry rot up under the eaves where it had snapped. The warp of fifty seasons had pulled the rusty old spikes out of the roofing timbers. The owner got too greedy. He thought he had a brand new two-car garage coming. He yammered too long and too loud about my plan to prop the sagging roof up on a new column and reshingle the corner area. It could have been done for about two hundred dollars.

The owner cheered up when I told him I'd changed my mind and I was willing to call it a total loss. I asked the contractor what he thought the structure was worth before the car smote it.

"Maybe fifty dollars," he said.

"Put it in writing, and I'll get another estimate."

The second estimate was seventy-five dollars. I told the owner I would approve a check to him for $62.50 for a total loss and he would receive it in due course.

He was still roaring at me as I drove away. I wished I could have continued the argument indefinitely. It was one way of being able to stop thinking too clearly about Sis Gantry. But alone in the car, traveling on roads too familiar, I had to endure the torment of my own worry, my special concern.

"Stupid broad!" I said, and hit the heel of my hand on the steering wheel. "Big, dumb, happy, generous broad!"

I caught the twelve o'clock news on the car radio. By the time they got down to the local news, I could have guessed how the news-hungry boys caught in the August doldrums were going to handle it.

"In the unexplained disappearance of Janice Gantry

last night, local police authorities do not discount the possibility that Miss Gantry could have been abducted by Charles Haywood, escaped safe-cracker believed to have been seen on Sunday night within five miles of Florence City. All highway patrol units have been alerted to look for Miss Gantry's car, a 1957 black Renault two door sedan bearing Florida license 99T313. Miss Gantry is twenty-nine years old, five-foot-ten inches tall, weighing approximately one hundred and forty-two pounds. She has black hair and dark blue eyes. When last seen she was wearing a maroon halter top, pale gray slacks and straw sandals, and she was carrying a straw purse with a floral design embroidered in yarn."

When he began talking weather I turned him off. I didn't need him to tell me it was going to be hot with a possibility of afternoon thunderstorms. The weather forecasts for every day from July 15th to September 15th on Florida's West Coast are exactly the same. Sometimes the storms threaten, but never quite get to you. Sometimes they hit early in the afternoon. Sometimes they hit late and last until midnight. It never changes.

I decided it was inevitable for the news people to tie the only two hot local stories together, to invent some link with or without evidence. I suspected I was the only one in the area, aside from Sis and Charlie, who knew how good the guess was—not abduction, but at least a joint effort—and neither of them would know that I knew. Charlie would have no special reason to tell Sis where he had found refuge. And it was out of character for the Sam Brice either of them knew to come lurking around, seeing them meet, following them. Following them up to that point when LeRoy Luxey put a hickory halt to the project.

If I had guessed right—if I had seen her phoning Charity Weber—then I had a ready-made starting place, if I could figure out what to do with it. For some reason I could not feel it would be a wonderful idea to go to the Weber house and ask if anybody had seen Sis and Charlie.

After a fast lunch in town I went out to the office and found a note for me to call Cal McAllen. I learned there was no news about Sis. The office was buzzing with excitement. People had been stopping in all morning, full of gossip, rumor and curiosity.

When I returned Cal's call, he asked me if it would be convenient for me to come to his office. He sounded hesitant and apologetic. I said I'd be over in a few minutes.

The law firm of Wessel and McAllen occupies a suite of offices on the fourth floor of the Florence City Bank and Trust Building. I had talked to Calvin McAllen five times that I could remember on matters connected with my little Automotive Appraisal Associates, and on three of those occasions it had been a phone conversation.

As I drove over I reviewed what I knew about him. He had been a highly successful corporation lawyer in Washington. About six years ago his wife had died very suddenly and unexpectedly of lukemia. He had resigned, liquidated all holdings that required careful watching, and retired to Florida at about 38 years of age, after stowing his two sons in private schools in the north. He had lived alone in a beach cottage for about a year, doing nothing, and then had suddenly taken the Florida bar exams and gotten his license to practice law. The town didn't pay any particular attention to him until he showed considerable shrewdness by going in with Wessel. You call him Hunk Wessel or Judge Wessel according to your station in life. He has more connections in three counties than any one man can use. Hunk isn't exactly crooked, but he is known to be very fast on his feet.

The girl at the front desk gave me a pretty smile and sent me right back through to Cal's office.

He stood up as I came in and said, "Good of you to come over, Sam. I appreciate it. I really do. Sit right there if you will. Would you try one of these cigars?"

"I'll stick to these, thanks, Cal."

He looked at me and moistened his lips and looked away again, and I knew he didn't know exactly where to start. The word 'colorless' suits him. He is middle-size, middle-height. He has fine textured grey hair, combed with precision, and a neutral face, gray eyes, and neat, tidy, unremarkable clothes. His voice is dry and level and

51

precise, his nails neatly kept. He could commit murder in front of forty witnesses and not a one of them would remember a thing about him. Because of my last talk with Sis, I could not help trying to draw a mental picture of the two of them in the marital sack. I could not make it plausible. I could not even imagine him with his hair uncombed.

"This is very difficult for me, Sam."

"You want to talk about Sis, don't you? Why should it be a strain? You're in love with her, aren't you?"

He squared his shoulders. "I have asked Janice to marry me."

"I think that's fine. But you didn't ask me here to give you my blessing."

"I've heard that . . . . you have known her very well." The poor guy was trying to be civilized and properly casual, but I could sense how much he would have enjoyed gutting me with a rusty machete.

I planned the words, then said, "Never fault her for that, Cal. We're good friends who like and respect each other. When the world had beaten us both flat, we got into an emotional thing, but that ended over two years ago because we found out we don't want the same things out of life. Nobody feels guilty or ashamed. Okay?"

"Nobody but me, right this minute," he said, with a smile that cost him dearly.

"She's steady and level and honest, Cal. Trust her, always."

"What I really want to ask you, Sam, is if you think this disappearance could be . . . my fault?" He continued quickly as he saw my look of bewilderment. "I'm an older man. She's a young girl. I've been pressuring her to make up her mind. Maybe she had to run away and give herself a chance to think it over."

"She is not a giddy young girl. She's twenty-nine, and all woman, and tough where it pays off. For God's sake, she spent four years married to a madman. He came within a sixteenth of an inch and thirty seconds of killing her when he killed himself. Run away? Sis walks right up to any problem that comes along and stares it square in the eye."

"I guess I keep trying to think of . . . reasons that won't scare me."

"She's a complete woman, and when she says yes, she's going to say it all the way, for keeps."

He picked up a long yellow pencil, studied it mildly, then abruptly snapped it in two and hurled the pieces into the wastebasket. "Then what the hell happened to her, Brice?"

"I don't know."

He swiveled his chair a quarter turn and looked out the wide window toward the blue bay. "When I lost Mary," he said in a tired voice, "I was certain I could not survive. But I did. I knew I would never want another woman. But now I do. I know now that I might survive the loss of Janice. But I do not like to think of what I might become without her." He turned back to me. "Do you know this Charles Haywood?"

"Yes. Not very well."

"Would he hurt her?"

"Not a chance of it. Maybe he's capable of hurting somebody if they hurt him. But not Sis. They're friends."

There was a sudden glint of shrewdness and speculation in his gray eyes. "Friends? I understand this Haywood has no family left here. If he wanted someone to help him, and he knew Sis, he might call her. She has such a great capacity for loyalty. He could have phoned her last evening. That could have been the call she got. It wasn't like her, Mrs. Gantry tells me, for her not to tell her people who had phoned. If it was Haywood, she wouldn't have told them the name."

It impressed me, that quickness and logic.

"So she took her car and picked him up. Then what, Cal?"

"This is the last place in the world Haywood should have come to. So he had some good reason. He had someone he wanted to see. She went with him, perhaps. And if harm came to him, it would not be safe to let her go. But who would he want to see?

"He tried to rob a man named Maurice Weber, Cal. Weber lives out near the south end of Horseshoe Key. Now this is only idle gossip I happened to hear, but at the time Charlie was sent up, there was a rumor around town that he was seeing Charity Weber. That's Mrs. Maurice Weber. There's a rumor the whole story never came out."

He thought for a few moments, then said, "Let's see what Millhaus has done. I'll put the call on the room mike so you can hear it."

He told his secretary to get the sheriff on the line. When the call came through it came out of a box like an intercom on McAllen's desk. Cal leaned back in his chair and answered in a normal tone of voice.

"Sorry to bother you again, Sheriff."

"Perfectly okay any time, Mr. McAllen. You know that."

"What I'm wondering now is if you've considered the possibility of Janice voluntarily helping this Haywood person?"

"Yes, I have. It wouldn't be a smart thing to do, but it would be the kind of thing Sis Gantry would do. He was a friend of some of her younger brothers and I guess she knew Charlie pretty well from him hanging around the house when they were all kids."

"In that case, have you thought of the possibility of Miss Gantry driving Haywood to the Weber house?"

"I thought of that, Mr. McAllen, and I was out there on the Key this morning to see the Webers. I figured that on account of Mr. Weber capturing Charlie, Charlie migh have come back to settle the grudge. Me and two of my deputies, we went all through the house and grounds. They got a good burglar alarm system and they went to bed early last night and they didn't hear a thing. In fact, Mr. Weber told me his wife had been a little nervous ever since they heard about Charlie escaping, and he wanted to know if I could spare a man to patrol around the house nights until Charlie is picked up. I said I could do that for him, so I'm putting Deputy Luxey out there beginning tonight."

"Well . . . thank you, Sheriff. It was just an idea."

I heard Pat's damp friendly chuckle. "You get any more of those ideas, Mr. Cal, you just let me know, hear?"

McAllen, after he pushed the button to break the connection, turned to me with a slight look of distaste. "Is that man any good?"

"He's average. There's better ones and worse ones, Cal."

"Who is this Maurice Weber?"

"Nobody knows much about him. He doesn't what you call mingle. Or his wife either. I think it was about four years ago a man whose name I can't remember came down and bought that piece of Gulf to bay land, four hundred feet of Gulf beach and bay frontage, about eight hundred feet deep. The land went for a hundred and ten thousand, I believe. That man had working drawings with him, and he put the job out on bid, and it went for a hundred and twenty-five thousand I think. He stayed right down and supervised the job, and let a contract for all the plantings and the boat basin and dock on the bay side. Just as everything was finished, a couple arrived in a big green Continental full of luggage and moved in. When a few neighbors tried to pay the usual call they got neatly brushed off. Mr. and Mrs. Weber had not arrived yet. The couple in residence were the servants who were getting the house ready. And when the Webers did arrive, it would perhaps be best not to pay any social calls, due to Mr. Weber's health."

"They apparently don't have to scrimp."

"You haven't heard it all. The agent furnished the house with the help of the servant couple. A man arrived with a fifty-four foot Matthews, brand new, and he turned out to be a combination boat captain and gardner, a rare and wonderful combination. When the whole place was ready, even to cut flowers and the beds turned down, I've heard, Mr. and Mrs. Weber appeared and moved in. And they've been there ever since."

"Where did they come from?"

"Michigan, I believe."

"What did he do?"

"The local word is that he was an investment banker."

"Are they old?"

"Yes and no. The few people who have gotten a good close look at him say he's in his middle fifties. His wife is supposed to be breathtaking, and in her early thirties."

"Haywood got friendly with her somehow?"

"That's the gossip."

"And then Mr. Weber caught him while he was trying to open a safe?"

"He wasn't trying to open it. It was set into the back of a closet in the dressing room off the master bedroom. He had a big pry bar. He was tearing the wall down. He apparently intended to pry the safe loose and carry it out. As I remember the story in the papers, it weighed less than a hundred pounds empty. It was a barrel job, small but damn sturdy."

"Everyone was away from the house?"

"It was late in the afternoon on a nice day in March, two years and four months ago. The Webers had gone out on the boat, with their hired captain. It was a Thursday, the house servants' day off. Presumably the servants had locked the house. But he had not broken in."

"And he knew exactly where the safe was."

"Yes."

"So he had either wormed that information out of the Weber woman, or she was in partnership with him."

"I thought you were in corporation law."

"The logic, or illogic of human behavior, Sam, has damn little to do with the law. Why wasn't all this brought out?"

"Who by, Cal? He made no fuss when they came and got him. He would permit no attempt to raise bail for him. He sat in a cell for three weeks until Circuit Court was in session, and he pleaded guilty and they sent him away."

"How come he got caught? I know all this was in the papers, but I paid no attention to it. I didn't know any of the people involved."

"He had bad luck. Ordinarily the servants wouldn't be back until ten o'clock. The Webers had left the dock right after lunch, planning to be back at about five-thirty. He admitted entering the house at quarter to three. He could see the boat basin from the window in the dressing room. He had parked the agency car he was using where it couldn't be seen from Orange Road or from their boat should they return earlier. But at about two-thirty one of

56

the diesels conked out on the boat. Weber had his man turn back and leave it at Jimson's Marina and stay with it to get it repaired. The Webers taxied home. They arrived a little after four. Charlie was too busy to hear the cab. Weber found the front door unlocked. When he walked in he heard somebody in the bedroom wing making a hell of a noise. He got a gun from his study and went in and caught Charlie hard at work. He disarmed him. Mrs. Weber called the law. And that was that. It was such a shock to Mrs. Weber that she took to her bed."

"She did indeed?" He stood up with a sudden restlessness. "But this gets us noplace. Millhaus has been out there. Janice is not . . . a devious sort of person."

"I can't get used to hearing her called Janice."

"Sis is an absurd name for her. It has a connotation of . . . sexlessness."

By a quick struggle I managed to squelch all the too obvious comments that drifted to the top of my mind. "I guess it does at that."

"She likes me to call her Janice. She says it makes her feel girlish and helpless."

"She's pulled too much weight too long. She needs somebody to lean on."

"I would very much like . . . that privileged position, Sam."

And right then he didn't look either cold or colorless. I saw more jaw than I had noticed previously, and his hands looked more powerful and capable than I would have guessed had I not noticed them.

He put one of those hands out and said, "I've disliked you intensely for months, Sam. Ever since she told me about . . . your affair."

"Wouldn't she, though? She's incapable of hiding anything. It was stupid to tell you, but it's her way of leveling."

"You're not the way I pictured you in this situation, Sam, so maybe none of it was the way I thought. You do value her?"

"Very much, Cal. She wants marriage, you know. And kids."

57

For half a moment he lost control of the shape of his mouth. "We've got to find her, Sam. And I don't know . . . what to do."

"I heard the local news. And I heard the news out of St. Pete. It's one of those things that people get excited about, Cal. The papers should be out soon. It'll be big. She's got hundreds of friends. There'll be a lot of pressure on the police to find her. A lot of people will be looking, Cal."

After I left Cal McAllen's office I knew it was time for one of my rare visits to D. Ackley Bush. I phoned him from my office desk.

"Samuel! For God's sake, my dear boy! Who am I to deny anyone willing to voluntarily expose himself to intelligent conversation? A meeting set for this evening has been canceled, so I am entirely free. I have been working again at my Yoga. Kishi is irreparably Oriental, but he seems to think it a kind of madness. He mutters and slams pots about. When can I expect you?"

"Five-thirty okay?"

"Splendid! The glasses will be chilled and ready."

It was almost exactly five-thirty when I turned into Ack's driveway. For the past thirty years—which would be approximately half his life—he has lived in the same bachelor beach house toward the south end of Horseshoe Key. When he came down and built it, there were only three cottages on the whole south half of the Key. A narrow causeway and a one lane plank bridge led out to the Key from the mainland. It was then very much the same as it had been when Caloosa Indians had encamped there, building their ceremonial mounds, unaware of the Spanish fist hovering over them. The interior of that house was one of the most vivid memories of my childhood, the crackle of fat pine in the fireplace of coquina rock, the leathery, musty smell of the books on rainy days, full of excitement, adventure, heroes.

Ack swung the door wide for me, beaming his pleasure. He is a round, pink, bouncing little man, with a Carl Sandburg thatch of white hair. He seems full of the scrubbed delight and harmless energy of a happy child, but there is a wicked light of irony in his bulging blue eyes which gives but faint warning of a tongue which serves him as mace, bludgeon, sabre and scalpel.

He herded me into the living room, like a range dog penning a seed bull, into that low-ceilinged place of books and paintings, sculpture and ceramics. The sepulchral, emaciated Kishi—who is somewhere between 38 and 108 —trudged in with the frosty treasure of the chilled Martini pitcher, gave me a rare smile that came and went so quickly I could not be certain I had not imagined it, filled the chilled glasses ceremoniously, and took the pitcher back out to put it on ice. I knew he would keep returning with it at those measured intervals he considered correct.

Ack said, "We were to meet to devise some new way to terrorize our County Commissioners, the poor things. But it had to be postponed. Are these dry enough for you, Samuel?"

"Just right. You're still up to here in the world's work, Ack?"

"Every gadfly do-gooder busybody board and committee within fifty miles. Somebody has to be tireless, my boy, or the fast buck operators would asphalt the entire coast, fill every bay and slay every living thing incapable of carrying a wallet. And with my left hand I strike the occasional blow of culture."

Suddenly the habitual animation in his face died away and he looked as morose as I had ever seen him. "But lately, Samuel, I have attacks of futility. Maybe there have been too many physical intimations of morality. I find myself wondering what the hell I have done with my life. I acquired too many graduate degrees too quickly and burned out a few little switches and came down here three decades ago to rest for one year, and write a book. I never finished it. I've even stopped mentioning it. The question of human function does open up a philosophical question as yet unanswered by the race—what is a valid pattern of existence? Thank God for the buccaneer ancestor who solved my money problems. I would have been very inept at making money, you know. These days I look around me and count failures. You are one of them, you know."

"Thanks so much, Doctor Bush."

"Seriously. The year you were born was the year I began renting your father's bay boat and his services as guide and captive audience. On one of his garrulous days, he would say three whole sentences. A marvelous man. He endured all the clatter of my compulsive chatter. He was amused by me. We became close and special friends in that curious way possible only to two men who have absolutely nothing in common."

"Except fishing."

"Ah, we killed monsters in those days! My regard for him was so high that I wished to open up the wide world of the mind and imagination to you, his only child. This is a most difficult task when the child is incurably muscular, good at games, gifted with the reflexes of a hungry weasel. But when you became old enough so that I could tell you had a good mind, flexible and sufficiently tough, I thought I had won the battle."

"This was the place to come on rainy days, Ack."

Kishi drifted silently in and refilled the long-stemmed glasses.

Ack shrugged. "A partial victory. I might have won. But when they were—drowned, both of them—you had just turned fifteen, hadn't you?"

"On Friday. They drowned on Sunday. I was supposed to go along, but I wanted to stay home and ride the motor bike he built for me."

"That was when I lost, Samuel. Thought became too painful for you. It was easier to find the exhaustion and sleep that came through the hard use of the brute muscle. So, in your muscle years, you lost your true image of yourself. You know that, I hope. You are an imposter, Samuel. You treat the world to a careful picture of the retired, slightly bitter professional athlete, large, insensitive, uncomplicated." He smiled. "It is such a waste, you know, playing a life role merely because it feels comfortable and undemanding. Growth is a function of conflict."

"I've had all the conflict I can use, Ack."

"At thirty? Really, my dear boy!"

60

"How much have you grown in thirty years?" I regretted it as soon as I said it. It inferred a contempt I did not feel. It categorized him as a ludicrous little man.

"Touché," he said, but his smile looked like a clever makeup job.

"I didn't mean that, Ack. You touched a sore spot, so I hit back."

"With excellent aim, my dear boy. I have a shallow, pyrotechnic, unchanging brilliance with which I awe the peasants, but there is no solidity, no basic texture, hence no capacity for creative growth. That is precisely why I never went back. I nearly destroyed myself trying to keep up with the Joneses in the academic world. Here, you see, I can be Jones. It is very satisfying. I never quite found the time to settle down and write the book which would have . . . established my basic triviality. I am in hiding, just as you are, but with better cause. Now that we have taken off our masks, my dear boy, we should be more at ease with each other."

"I don't like to hear you low rate yourself, Ack."

"Don't sit there glooming at me like a ruptured buffalo, Samuel. I am not emotional about my defects, I assure you. When I feel inadequate, I merely go out and harpoon some public official, winch him up onto dry land and gut him in public. It's a cruel pastime, but mine own. This month, in a sublime exercise of stupidity, they are trying to quietly turn over a public park to the State Road Department, an organization dedicated to stamping out every green and growing thing. We shall flay them briskly, salt them down and then, on their promise to behave, give them permission to climb back into their own skins, like donning winter underwear."

I could see that through a determined effort he was regaining his good spirits. "I have come to you, Ack, because you know everything about everybody."

The comment delighted him. "It's all very simple, my dear boy. I have insatiable curiosity, an infallible memory, uncomparable persistence and a fondness for intrigue and espionage. And thirty years of exercising these talents locally, remember. But I am not a common gossip. I am an uncommon gossip. I store up the best tidbits so I can

61

use them to implement my civic projects. I prefer to call it well-organized blackmail."

"Do you know that Sis Gantry is missing and the police are looking for her?"

He was surprised and shocked by the news. He hadn't heard any newscasts or seen the evening paper, and for once, no one had called him. As I started to tell him an edited version of the whole thing, I suddenly realized that I was going to feel a lot better if I told someone the complete story. So I paused and started to go back to the very beginning of it, which was my relation with Sis . . .

"We can skip all that history, Samuel. I am aware of the precise period when you were indulging yourself with the almost too obvious charms of that husky maiden, and I suspect that under the circumstances it was a theraputic venture for both of you. The Gantry family was indignant, but fortunately you and the lady went at it in such a sensibly private and circumspect way that you never had to discuss it with her pack of muscular brothers. And you two were capable of ending the romp without ending the friendship, a rare and refreshing sign of mutual maturity."

"How the hell would you . . ."

"Even the Florence County raccoons are in my service, dear boy. Please continue."

I enjoyed astonishing him with the report of Charlie Haywood's visit. I covered every significant event, including my association with LeRoy Luxey and my talk with Cal McAllen. Kishi's fourth silent visit made me aware of a slight numbness around the mouth, a familiar syndrome based on Ack's martini formula. The Gulf rested silently against the white beach. The sun was down and, through the panes of the large casement window I could see a small patch of the sea, gray-purple in what was left of the light, stretching out to a narrow crimson band across the horizon.

"It is a complex equation," Ack said, "with so many factors missing it cannot yet be solved, but we can have the inescapable feeling that the answer, when we find it, will bear a relation to the Weber menage."

"Your neighbors?"

"Not exactly. They are a quarter-mile south of here.

And not exactly neighbors of anyone, Samuel. The semantics of the word imply some form of human contact. A morning nod, at least. But even that is missing."

"Ack, do you know anything about them?"

"Do I know anything *useful* about them? This intrigues me enormously, Samuel. I have tried to focus my lense upon them. They are a challenge. They have a fetish for privacy. It has the stature of mania. The house and grounds and plantings were designed to achieve maximum privacy. They have been in residence a little less than four years. They have slept in that house every night, so far as I know. They have gone nowhere. The mode of existence is abnormal, to say the least. Most abnormal for monied people. I can tell you some odd things."

"If you ever get around to it, Ack."

He ignored me. He had gotten up to pace thoughtfully back and forth in a restricted area between crowded bookshelves. He was in his habitual costume for all informal events, a Churchillian jump suit with D.A.B. embroidered on the breast pocket. This one was slate blue. He mailorders them from some California outfit, and has them in all possible shades.

"Mail, for example. They receive a wide range of magazines, but not one of them is specialized, indicative of any field of interest. And they get the junk mail, of course. The circulars. Early each month Mr. Weber receives a registered letter, special delivery, from Chicago. About twice a month Mrs. Weber receives a personal letter addressed in a female hand, mailed from Richmond, Virginia. They receive no other mail. Have they no friends, relatives, business contacts?"

"The question is rhetorical."

"Finances. Land and construction were paid for by cashier's check drawn on a Chicago Bank. They maintain no local bank account. The servants pay all local bills in cash. Even when he purchased a second automobile . . ."

"I heard about that. It made people think Charlie was after the cash."

"But you don't think so?"

"Maybe he was after the cash, but not for the obvious reasons. I don't know. Keep talking."

"They do not entertain local people and are not entertained by them. They never eat out. Aside from the very rare trips into town—such as the time the car was purchased—they leave the house only to go out on that boat. Such secrecy is a challenge to me, Samuel."

"Of course."

"And so I took the obvious course—cultivation of the servants. Their boat captain was hired in Miami. He never laid eyes on the Webers until he arrived here. He is a competent, silent, self-sufficient man. He hates women and worships boats and shrubs. It took weeks of care and guile to learn next to nothing. He is well paid. The Webers are good people to work for. When they are on the boat, they are quiet. They have very little to say to each other. He gets his room and board and a salary monthly in cash. Mr. Weber computes the withholding tax and the social security, and when it has to be paid, the other man servant buys postal money orders in the right amount and sends it in.

"The couple is named Mahler. Herman and Anna. They are a middle-aged German couple. They saw enough of violence in World War Two to want only a placid, quiet, comfortable life. They are hopelessly content in this job. And they, too, never met the Webers until they were here on the Key. They were employed through a New York agency and interviewed by a man they have not seen since. They were delighted to hear my very bad German. Here is their report. The Webers are very nice people. They never quarrel. Mrs. Weber does not cook or plan meals. She reads magazines, watches television and swims in the pool. Mr. Weber reads magazines, watches television, swims in the pool and plays solitaire. They go to bed early. The attempted robbery was a terrible thing. The Webers were very upset about it."

"Ack, does anybody ever come to see them from out of town?"

"Good question. Yes. Men. Sometimes one. Sometimes two. But it's always the same two men. They come down about every three months, and stay two or three days. They fly down from the north and drive down from Tampa or Sarasota in a rented car, and leave the same way. Oh, and there are two private unlisted phones. One is used for local calls, to stores and so forth. Anna Mahler, who is in the main part of the house most of the day, has never heard the other one ring."

"It sounds," I said, "like one hell of a quiet life."

"I admitted defeat at least a year ago, Samuel. Things may have changed at the Weber house, but I doubt it. Do you know what they look like?"

"I've seen them, Ack. When I've been out on the boat, I've seen that Matthews of theirs come along the channel, and out of curiosity I've put the glasses on them. What's the name of that cruiser?"

"The *Sea Queen*. It's one of those damnable names, so ordinary it slips right out of the mind."

"In good weather she likes to sit up at the bow. In a swim suit she's worth the long look with the glasses."

"She's a gloriously lovely woman. You've looked at Maurice Weber too?"

I shrugged. "I wouldn't know him if I saw him on the street. Heavy, slightly swarthy, thick dark gray hair."

"I've seen him just enough times to notice something very odd about him, my boy." Ack sat in his chair again and gave me that look which warned me I should soon applaud his cleverness. "Money, Samuel, works a curious transformation on any man. When you have had money long enough, it works its gentle magic for all the world to see. It affects dress, posture, carriage, the modulations of the voice, even the way you light a cigarette or lift a drink. It enables the happy possessor thereof to radiate a quiet confidence, a not unpleasant self-esteem.

"I could not pin down what it was that bothered me about Maurice Weber until one day I happened to see him walking from his Gulf beach toward his driveway gate, and he had the same manner that those people have who trespass around this neighborhood during the summer. There is a manner of arrogant apology about the man. A great interpretive dancer might walk that way to express insecurity, suspicion, and a sort of peasant surliness. Money has made no mark upon him."

"Aren't you getting pretty far out?" I asked him.

"We must consider our instincts in all things. And

you must remember, Samuel, that this couple have not been so conspicuous in their insistence on privacy that they have defeated their own purpose. It's been cleverly done. They've not excited the curiosity of the community."

"Yours."

"But I am uniquely nosey, my boy. On the whole nobody knows them, or gives a damn about knowing them. If the Haywood incident hadn't come up, the anonymity would be almost complete and perfect. I am suspicious and a cynic."

"And so?"

"And so it has all been too cleverly planned to be accidental. It is neither a normal use of money, nor a way of living that could be a matter of free will."

"But how about the people we are always reading about who die alone in houses full of fifty years of junk, with millions in the bank."

"A type The eccentric recluse. Withered, suspicious, less than sane. Spinsters of both sexes, Samuel." He finished the final quarter-inch of martini. "These Webers are not of that breed. Neither of them have the look of the introvert. But, bless me, I can think of no plausible reason for their . . masquerade."

"They robbed a bank."

"In the curious illogic of a television script, that might be acceptable. But this is the era of IBM, of records, card files, the implacable assignment of identification numbers to this and that. Certainly the size of the land transaction and the construction project would come to the attention of earnest little men in Jacksonville. And they would want some assurance that our Mr. Weber was entirely clean with Internal Revenue. If you have successfully looted a bank, it is a very poor time to indulge yourself in conspicuous consumption. We must assume a certain degree of legitimacy, wouldn't you say?"

"I . . . guess so, Ack."

"If we can continue to believe that the sudden disappearance of Miss Gantry is linked in some way to the unknown status of the Webers, then it becomes imperative to learn more about the Webers."

"So I take a try at the safe?"

"Sometimes you are discouragingly dull, Samuel."

"It was like a joke."

"Where did young Charlie start?"

"What? Oh, with the wife."

"And if that is the area of vulnerability, it could work again."

"Sure, Ack. I'll ring the doorbell and ask for her. When I get a chance I give her the big wink, like this. And the leer. And I say, 'How about it, chick?'"

He gave me a look of frosty impatience. "Is all this just a trivial thing to you?"

"I'm scared, Ack. I'm scared to death about Sis. Millhaus and his boys tramped through the Weber house. There doesn't seem to be anywhere to go from here. I keep thinking she'll turn up with a plausible excuse. But that's just pollyanna, and I know it. So I make funnies because I'm a little clutched. The guy with the spear through the gut saying it hurts only when he laughs. What I *really* want to do is go the hell home and forget it." I could feel the martinis, trying to talk.

"So go home, Samuel," he said.

"I can't."

"You don't owe anything to anybody. Isn't that your design for living, dear boy? Non-involvement? They wouldn't let you climb the apple tree any more, so you went home to sulk. Coming back to life can be too painful."

"Get off me, Ack. For Chrissake."

"I want you to see that you cannot toy with a partial involvement. Get in all the way or get out all the way."

I did not answer him. All the light was gone. I could no longer see his face. Kishi came in and turned on two lamps with dark red shades. "Ritter time before chow," he announced.

After he left the room I said, "I won't drag my feet, Ack."

"All the Gulf beaches below the high tide mark belong to all the people, Samuel. Mrs. Weber swims alone at dawn. At other times she uses their private pool. The only other times I have ever seen her on the beach is

after a storm stooping and pouncing with that particular
avidity characteristic of the shell collector. My abortive
attempts to strike up a conversation went over like a
clay glider."

He went over to a glass-front case to the left of the
fireplace, selected a shell and brought it back and handed
it to me. It was about three inches across, conical, black
with gaudy blotches of white.

"This one should do," he said. "We must assume that
extreme rarity would make her suspicious, if she knows
anything about shells. And you will see that this one is
not perfect. It's a magpie, or *livona pica*. It is very abun-
dant as a Pleistocene fossil, but more rare now. Of course
it is much too clean. You'll have to soak it in salt water
and pack it with beach sand. You can give it to her, if
it seems to work."

"The shell game," I said.

"Plus your primitive charm, of course. Is beefcake in
the proper argot? Women are supposed to have a special
primordial response to any male who looks capable of
slaying a saber-toothed tiger with a stone-age ax."

"LeRoy Luxey would weigh about one hundred and
twenty-nine, club and all."

"Chow," Kishi said firmly.

Chapter Five

I SPENT THE first two hours of Wednesday morning on D. Ackley Bush's hundred feet of Gulf beach, fuddling around in a faded old pair of swim trunks, feeling conspiratorial and foolish. Along the gentle crescent of the beach I could see the emptiness of the beach in front of the Weber place. The only soul I saw was a leathery old man two hundred yards north of me, spincasting with timeless patience.

At eight o'clock I went back into Ack's yard, rinsed off the salt under his outside shower, toweled and changed in the angle between my car and a pepper hedge, stowed my *livona pica* in the glove compartment. Ack came out and I gave him the negative report and thanked him again for a good evening. I assured him I wasn't going to give up after only one blank morning

My morning mail confirmed the lull in my one-man operation. When accidents are bad enough, I do not enter the picture. There had been a dandy in the night, over on State Road 565 near Ravenna, a classic head on on a curve, killing seven, including one guy I had met casually, Troy Jamison, a builder from Ravenna, who had come down and married local money and started some kind of big development down there. From the front page photo in my morning paper, I could see that if one of my client companies had insured either of those vehicles, all I'd have to do would be approve the scrap price.

On this morning I became aware of a change in attitude toward Sis's disappearance. It wasn't a big enough case for nationwide or even statewide coverage, but it was a hot item on our coast, from Everglades City to Tarpon Springs. Somehow the attention seemed to blur the remembered image of Sis Gantry. She was becoming oddly fictional, an actress in a play. Normal office routine had become impossible. Even with the inevitable reduction of work, Alice Jessup could not handle the entire secretarial routine. Vince Avery had wired Tom Earle in Canada, and Vince was hanging around the office waiting for Tom to put a call through to him.

I heard that Scotty Gantry, the eldest son, had canceled his vacation plans and driven down with his family from Atlanta to be with his parents. Scotty located me at four-thirty that afternoon in the gloom of Gus Herka's Best Beach Bar. He had stopped at the office and they had told him where he could find me.

With no hypocrisy of greeting or handshake he said, "Wanna talk to you, Brice," and led the way over to a far table by the bowling machine.

He is nearing forty. He is wide, tough, deliberate and aggressive—a vice president and sales manager of a growing company that makes plastic and fiberglass boats.

"What do you know about this, Brice?"

"Absolutely nothing."

"She talked to you Monday night."

"Not Monday night, Scotty. Monday evening. In the office. Where did you get your information?"

"At dinner she said something to Mom about talking to you, something so casual Mom can't remember what she said. So what were the two of you talking about?"

"Nothing that could have anything to do with what's happened."

"I'll decide what's pertinent and what isn't. What did you talk about?"

"You're the big brother, taking care. Don't lean on me, Scotty."

"You want to step out the back door a minute?"

"Grow up. Neither of us has been eighteen for a long long time."

"I want to know what you talked about."

I couldn't help the audible sigh. "It was a private conversation. She hasn't made up her mind about marrying

Cal McAllen. We were talking about that. She's about decided to say yes. Every family can use a lawyer, I guess."

"Better she should marry any son of a bitch in the state than you."

"She married so damn good the first time?"

"Nobody could stop her."

"Were you going to try to stop her this time?"

"Why the hell should we?"

"Nobody in the world is good enough for your kid sister, Scotty."

"I sure as hell know you're not. A lawyer, okay. Not a crooked ballplayer."

"For something that never got into the papers, that got a lot of circulation, Scotty."

"It's hard to hide dirt."

"If I gave a damn for your opinion one way or the other, I'd take the time to tell your story."

"Your version. No thanks. I'd dearly love to jolt you around some, Brice."

"You've got a lot of hostility there, boy."

"Sis was just getting back on her feet when you moved in on her with a lot of big talk. She always thinks everybody is just fine. You set her way back, Brice. You moved in on her when her guard was down."

"Do you think I hurt her? Honestly?"

"You used her. And when you got tired of her, you broke it off. You think you did her any good?"

I can think of forty ways I could have answered that question more diplomatically. But my patience was worn thin. His manner was irritating.

"I guess I must have done her some good, pal. She used to scream with joy."

He trotted heavily to the rear door and held it open, yelling vast incoherencies at me. I had obligated myself, and so I went blinking out into a sunny ash can arena. I caught three wild and violent swings on my arms, timed the fourth one, trapped his wrist, twisted it up between his shoulder blades and ran him headlong into the side of the frame building. The vice-president and sales manager dropped loosely onto his face. I rolled him onto his back. He was in the shade. He was snoring. His pulse was strong and regular. He stopped snoring, swallowed, opened his eyes and looked up at me.

"Take a little rest before you try to get up."

"Baasard," he mumbled.

I went back inside, picked my beer off the table and went back to the bar. "Awful goddam quick, you know it?" Gus said. "One big thump on the building, and here you are. I don't go out ever on account of blood turns my stomach."

"No blood," I said. I rubbed my left arm. He had numbed it a little.

"He still out there, Sam?"

"Maybe."

"Some tourist could take his shoes and money, you know it?"

I finished my beer and walked back and looked. Scotty was gone. I went back and told Gus and he seemed relieved.

That evening I received my punishment for working off my frustration at Scotty Gantry's expense. I had gone to bed, after setting the alarm early enough to give me time to get over to the damn beach. I was leafing through a magazine. There was an article on Hawaii, with colored photographs. I turned a page and Judy smiled out at me. It was like forgetting you have pleurisy and trying to take a deep breath. But all the pain was in the heart.

She wore a blue swim suit, spangled with stars. She sat on a hatch cover in the sunshine, smiling happily into the lense. Water droplets stood on the honeyed perfection of her shoulders. A towhead about a year and a half old was leaning against her thigh, beaming up at her. Behind her I could see a section of ships railing, blue water, and a tropical shoreline.

"Mrs. Timothy Barriss Falter, the former Judy Caldwell, and one of the most charming young hostesses in the Islands, is shown here with her daughter, Gretchen aboard the family schooner, *Halekulani Girl*. Tim Falter, one of the best known architects in Hawaii, often entertains friends and clients aboard the schooner, with the help of his lovely wife, by taking cruises to the outlying islands. The schooner, which sleeps ten in addition to crew quarters for captain, mate and steward, was built in California two years ago to Mr. Falter's specifications."

I knew she was out there. I had heard her married name, but I had managed to forget it, an exercise in amnesia I would be unable to perform twice.

"—the former Judy Caldwell—"

Not the former Mrs. Sam Brice No mention of three years and three months of marriage to Sam. I had been expunged from the record It put me in the category of a childhood disease. She had had measles, whooping cough and Brice's disease.

I knew how gratified her imperious little father felt about the way things had worked out. He had faced the fact of our elopement with the same joy and understanding he would have displayed if he had found out she had been carted off to a tree house by an ape. After he had wheeled a battalion of lawyers into battle formation, she was able to forestall annulment only by convincing him she would kill herself if he pressed it through. He did not give up until after he had sent a man to see me, a dim, spindly, hesitant man bearing a check with so many zeros it gave me vertigo to look at it. But she was worth that amount per minute.

But after the inconceivable lapse of marrying me, she had steadied back onto course, regaining the lost image.

She stared at me out of the sunshine, with a Kodak smile. I threw the magazine against the wall and turned out the light, but she was still there, smiling.

"You see, Sam," she said. "It's all right with me now. I'm sorry about us. But I have what I must have. I guess I loved you, but you couldn't keep up the payments. You wouldn't have wanted what I would have become."

As long as I was drawing my pay, shrewd little Damon Caldwell had kept up his daughter's hefty allowance. It was more than I was getting for having my brains clouted loose every Sunday. Hers all went for clothes, cars, fun and half the rent. Mine picked up the slack. But when they threw me out, the shrewd little bastard cut her off. Maybe he even smiled while doing it, if he was sure a smile wouldn't fracture his teeth.

She clung to me and wept wildly and said the world couldn't lick us. She would scrub floors, wait on tables, wear rags. Maybe if we'd had kids . . . But we'd agreed they were for later, because they'd cut down our fun life. A month later, after being restless, bitchy and violent, she packed and went home to Wilmington, claiming she would rejoin me after I got located. (I was still running doggedly through my list of fair weather friends.)

I got a sprawled, unpunctuated, confusing letter from her, averaging ten words to the page. I flew to Wilmington. In a frenzy of tears she told me she was no good, had no character, couldn't love a poor man. I gathered she was either going to kill herself, go into a convent, take acting lessons, become a model, devote her life to good works, write a sensitive novel or take up nursing. But she made it clear that whatever she did, I wasn't in the picture. She wept out her guilt and shame. She fled. The princess went back into the castle and they yanked up the drawbridge.

My next communication was from a Nevada lawyer. I knew then how completely they had whipped me, so I came home for good. It seems to be standard practice to do that. You make them stop the world and let you off, or you go home.

As the morning world was turning from gray to gold on Thursday morning, and a bank of mist was rising from the gun-metal water, I looked south along the beach and saw a distant manikin, limber and moving well, unmistakably female at even twice that range, walk down to the water and stand knee deep to make the final adjustment of a bright yellow swim cap, then wade and plunge and begin swimming straight out, in the sleek, slow, powerful cadence that can be achieved only through lessons and work and a desire for excellence.

So I began to make the motions of the shell collector, moving down the brittle windrow at the high tide line, dropping plausible items in the paper sack I was carrying, trying to move at the pace which would guarantee the stylized interception. She floated out there, and I knew

that when she looked toward shore she could not fail to
see me. There was a continual increase in the heat of
the sun on my shoulders.

Soon I was within fifteen feet of the towel she had
dropped. A bushy salmon-pink towel, a new pack of Vice-
roys, a narrow gold lighter, a pair of sunglasses with yellow plastic frames. I made like a sheller working a fruitful
area. She started in. I did not resume forward movement
until I heard the sloshing as she was wading out. I did
not look at her.

I watched her bare tan feet as she crossed my bows,
perhaps eight feet away. Nice feet. Tan and narrow with
a high arch.

"Excuse me," I said, standing up, reaching into my
paper sack and fumbling for the *livona pica*, and looking
at all the rest of her.

There is one demon loose upon the world who spends
all his infinite time and energy on the devising of all
the vicious little coincidences which confound mankind.
His specialty is to confront the unwary with coincidences
so eerie, so obviously planned by a malevolent intelligence, that time itself comes to a full stop and his victim
stands transfixed by a conviction of unreality, while in
infra-space, the demon hugs his hairy belly, kicks his
hooves in the air, rolling and gasping with silent laughter.

The busy demon had clad this woman in a strapless
swim suit of lavender-blue, spangled with stars. It was a
perfect copy of the one Judy was wearing in the color
picture in the magazine. The morning sun touched the
water droplets on her golden shoulders. I knew at once
that this one was Judy's height—to the half-inch—her
weight to the quarter-pound. The build was the same,
short-waisted, long-legged. It was a figure without that
mammillary opulence which has become a fetish in the
entertainment business. A fool, with a hasty glance,
might get an impression of boyishness. But even a fool
would have the compulsion to look once more and would
see then all the tidy limber gifts, the structural intricacy.

The glutton can please himself with a hearty, simple
dish; the gourmet requires a perfect blending of tastes,
something to savor and remember, never totally identi-

fiable. Man never becomes sated with mystery.

So I stood like a fool, gawping at her. It was not Judy's face or her hair. But the textures of her and the way she stood and even her expression were so much like Judy that I had the grotesque conviction, for a few seconds, that it was all an elaborate joke. They had used makeup. They had trapped me. Now they would all come popping out of the bushes to laugh at me.

But it was not Judy. If Judy was flawed in any way, it was because there was a faint—a very faint suggestion of sharpness about her features. This girl was flawed in an opposed way—her features snubbed, subtly heavy—a broader mouth, heavier brows, higher, sturdier cheekbones, more roundness in her face. There was more boyishness in this girl's face, more merriness perhaps. This girl's eyes were a clear, pale, startling green. Her hair looked to be of coarser texture than Judy's. It was an ashy silver, a color nature could hardly have accomplished, yet close enough to her own so that it did not look at all lifeless. It was a casual cut, fairly short, yet avoiding that skinned look the Italians have foisted on an unwary world. I remembered Gus's comment about floozy hair, and knew he could have made it only because he had not seen this girl up close.

I suddenly realized that the local estimate of her age was considerably off—or else she was a marvelously youthful item for a woman in her early thirties as had been reported to me.

I could not have stood there like an idiot for more than a few seconds, but it was a few seconds too long. She managed to look both alarmed and amused.

"Excuse me," I said again, and I took the *livona pica* out of my brown paper bag and moved a step closer and held it out and said, "I wondered if you might know what this one is."

She shook her head. "It's a shell. That's as far as I can go. Flashy, isn't it?" It was a furry, husky little voice.

You could collect shells, I guessed, without knowing the names. Crows and pack rats collect shiny things without looking them up in catalogues. She dipped her face into the big towel.

"This is the first one of these I've found," I said inanely.

"That's nice," she said with a total indifference, and I knew she was going to pick up bathing cap, sunglasses and cigarettes and walk away from me. Such a girl would have become expert in fending off the casual pass. I searched for something to say, but everything I could think of sounded like just another dull attempt to strike up a conversation.

"I thought you might have found one of these," I said.

She made no answer. That makes it particularly difficult. She picked up the bathing cap, sunglasses and cigarettes. She started toward the path through the sea oats.

"I can wiggle my ears," I said desperately.

She stopped and half turned to look at me over her shoulder. "What?"

"The shell didn't work worth a damn. I can't see where yelling fire would get me anywhere. You brought sunglasses and cigarettes, so you were going to spend a little while on the beach, but you ran into a pest with a paper bag full of shells so you changed your mind. Okay, so I'm a pest. But I really can wiggle my ears and twenty years ago it was my only social grace. I was a very rabbity looking child."

She turned all the way back toward me, stifling a smile, marched three paces toward me and said, "It's something I don't see every day. Go ahead."

"Which one?"

"Selective control, huh? The left one."

I turned the left one toward her. I flexed the proper muscles.

"That's pretty tricky," she said.

"Want to see the right one now?"

"When you've seen one, you've seen them all."

"I am legitimately a pest, but I reacted in a way that couldn't help driving you away. The way I stared at you. I'm not a cretin, really. You look so much like somebody I . . . used to know that I had a sort of temporary paralysis."

"You boggled."

77

"I'm sorry. I'm a legitimate resident of Florence City. I own my own business and my own bachelor cottage. Your neighbor just up the road, Dr. D. Ackley Bush, can tell you I am a reasonably respectable man with voting rights and so on. What I'm saying is you should give a pest a chance to function. Or he gets frustrated. You can pick your own topic of conversation. I could tell you, for example, about an albino raccoon who used to live back there where your house is nearly twenty years ago. You know, folklore, nature talks."

She hesitated. "And you do collect shells?"

I dumped the contents of my paper bag back into the tidal windrow from which they had come. "Hardly," I said. "I'll keep this one because it is unusual. I think it's a magpie shell. The shell routine was a ploy. But it was the best thing I could think of. Unless, of course, you'd like this one."

She smiled and moved down to the flat tidal sand and spread the big towel. "You keep it. If you'd said you actually collect shells, I'd be across the road by now. Somehow you're not the type." She sat on her towel and put her sunglasses on and frowned up at me. "But wasn't it a pretty labored kind of routine?"

"Walking up and saying hello is pretty arrogant. I think you should have some kind of stage management." She offered me a cigarette. I sat on my heels and leaned forward to the guttering lighter flame in her cupped hand.

"Actually, the albino raccoon is much better bait. Tell me about him."

"Her. And her name was Mrs. Lot, given to her by D. Ackley Bush."

"Mrs. Lot? Oh. Lot's wife, of course."

"Ack was feeding them. He still does, but the raccoon population on the Key has gone way down since the Key has gotten so built up. Stupid people classify them as vermin and keep hollering about getting rid of them."

"I love them dearly. Thieves in black masks."

"They're a bright and rewarding animal. A half-dozen or so used to appear on Ack's back porch just after dark every night to be fed. If he wasn't on the job they'd raise hell, rattling the door latches, climbing trees and peering

78

in the windows complaining about his sudden neglect. She showed up with the group one night and became a steady customer.

"I was ten or eleven. He told my family about it and I used to come over on my bike to see her. They get very tame once they have confidence in you. Chicken skin is a special delicacy. She would take it out of my hand. Shy, dignified and fastidious. Not with her teeth. She'd reach out and take it with her hand."

"How nice."

"Then she changed her habits. She would grab the food and run, come back and get more and run, and finally return and eat the way she used to."

"Babies?"

"That was Ack's conclusion. She'd make a beeline south, and he estimated from the elapsed time that she lived in the big tangle of live oaks that stood where your house now stands. And finally one night she didn't show up until the others had eaten and gone. She made such a racket on the back porch that Ack came out. She had two half-grown offspring with her, both of normal pigmentation. When they tried to run from Ack she gave them both a good thumping. She hung back while they ate, then she ate and took the kids back home."

"Proud?"

"I saw her twice with the younguns. Not so much pride as a sort of complacency, a quiet air of self-satisfaction. And it wasn't long before she had them taking their chances along with the whole group. No special protection. Suddenly she stopped appearing with the group. Ack was worried about her. One day, a little over a week later, he was walking along Center Street over in town and he found her. She was in the window of a tackle store over there. The owner, a pretty good amateur taxidermist had . . ."

"Oh, no!"

"Mrs. Lot was posed on a piece of limb glaring with glass eyes, showing her needle fangs in a snarl that, as Ack said, cast a slur on her disposition."

The girl turned her head away from me just then and I could see her in profile, see, behind the sunglasses, the

79

big tear shimmering on her lashes. Could this be a sinister person? Yet history records many sentimental murderers.

"The taxidermist was so proud of his job he had put it in his window until the customer came to pick it up. Ack learned that Mrs. Lot had been brought in by a commercial fisherman named Prail, and had been shot through the head with a small caliber gun. Ack told my father. My father remembered telling Prail about Mrs. Lot. My father was a large, silent, gentle man. But Prail was larger, and twelve years younger. My father went to see Prail. Prail admitted stalking and killing Mrs. Lot, in spite of the county ordinance against shooting at any wild life on the Key. He hoped to be able to sell her to a tourist for a good price. My father solemnly and methodically whipped Wilbur Prail. He stopped a little bit this side of killing him. My father went to Prail's shack and retrieved Mrs. Lot and left the taxidermy fee on the table, plus five cents for the bullet. He gave her back to Ack who pried her off the limb and buried her behind his house. When Prail got out of the hospital he tried to organize a little group to work my father over but by then everybody knew the story and Prail could find nobody with any enthusiasm for the project. It was something he did not wish to try all by himself."

The girl shoved her cigarette into the sand. She said, with a small catch in her voice, "That's a nice joyful story. Can you think of any more ways to depress me?"

"I should have invented a new ending, I guess."

"No. This one is all right in some ways. I like paying for the bullet."

"There isn't any moral. Except, maybe, if you are too unusual, you may turn into a collector's item."

"When the Martians arrive I hope they go around collecting people and stuffing them."

"It will serve them right."

She smiled in a rueful way. "I guess I did sound pretty fierce. How can you sit like that so long?"

"It's a local custom among us poor folks. When you visit a man, you don't go set in his house. You hunker in the yard and whittle."

She stood up and pulled her rubber cap on. "I've got

to swim away from that darn raccoon of yours."

I went into the water when she was a hundred feet out. I lazed along, knowing exactly how bad I would look if I got into any sort of contest with her. I churn along without grace, style or speed. I can keep it up all day, but it will never win any medals. She had that competition look, the stroke that goes with those racing turns against the end of an Olympic pool.

I raised my head and saw her fifty feet further out loafing on her back. I went on out and rolled to float beside her.

"Darn it," she said, "that white raccoon is going to haunt . . ." She gave a sudden gasp of pain and surprise. She had been utterly at home in the water, but suddenly she began to flounder and struggle.

I went under fast to take a look at her. Sometimes we get a psychotic sand shark or nurse shark in Gulf waters. It is a very rare thing. They then confound the ichthyologists by chomping at anything that floats or moves. But the clear water was empty. I could see the pattern of sand ripples on the bottom some twelve feet down. Her right leg was bent sharply at the knee, with her foot curled and twisted, her calf muscles bulged and knotted.

I popped up beside her. She looked gray under her tan but I could see she wasn't going to panic. She was trying to smile. "Cramp," she said.

"And a real dandy. First class."

"Golly! It hurts." And the hurting wrenched the attempt at a smile off her face.

I towed her in. I towed her along on her back by my one hand cupped under her chin, sidestroking with my right arm and doing big froggy kicks. When I got her into the shallows she got up onto her good leg, but she couldn't hop through knee-deep water. I swung her up and carried her up the incline of the beach and put her down on the big towel and said, "Roll onto the tummy."

I knelt beside her right leg. "Now make a big effort to relax the muscles."

"I never had anything hurt just like this," she said in a small voice.

The calf was bunched and ugly, and like marble to the touch. Her foot was curled like a ballet dancer, and turned

81

inward. I began to knead the hard ball of muscle exerting pressure to straighten her leg out as I did so. She whimpered once. In about sixty seconds I felt the first slackening of tension and I was able to get the leg down a little. Soon I had the leg flat. The calf muscles jumped and quivered as the cramp knots softened. The ugliness went away and once again the calf was as it should be, long, rounded, supple—a slim leg made for dancing and running and joy. As I had expected, the foot had begun to look a lot letter. I massaged it, working at the arch with my thumbs until the muscle hardness was gone.

She gave a long and comfortable sigh. "It feels so good when it goes away. Can I sit up now?"

"Now you stand up, and we walk off what's left."

She limped quite badly for the first twenty paces, and I walked slowly beside her on the packed sand. But as the limp diminished, she began to stride along in better form.

"I've had little leg cramps before. Never anything like that."

"People think if you wait an hour after eating, no cramps. They're right, about stomach cramps. But your leg can go any time. Or both of them. It's sort of a rebellion of the nerves. So swimming alone is about like standing under a tall tree in a thunderstorm."

"It would be a little exaggerated and phoney to thank you for saving my life. I could have gotten to shore."

"I know you could. You're so at home in the water you could have subdued any panic and backstroked your way in, not using our legs, floating when you got tired. But it was easier this way."

"That's for darn sure!"

"How does it feel now?"

"Just a little twinge every time my weight comes down on it, but even that is going away."

"If you swim again today there's the off-chance it'll come back. But you'll be okay tomorrow."

"Is this far enough?" she asked. I nodded and we turned and headed back toward the bright spot of the towel far down the beach.

I was very conscious of her walking beside me, and I didn't want to look at her. I'd had about all I could handle. I had kneaded that perfect golden texture of her, feeling the warmth and aliveness of the long flat muscles. It was all so vividly reminiscent of Judy that I felt too close to doing some wildly improbable, unpredictable thing. I had wanted to kiss the tender hollow behind her knee. The memory of the weight of her in my arms was too specific. I hated Maurice Weber for his ownership of this precious entity.

"I would not care to drown, thank you," she said.

I should have made some comment in the same casual, bright vein, and I intended to, but when I opened my mouth I heard myself say, "My parents drowned in the Gulf when I was fifteen."

"How horrible!"

"It was a long time before I could believe it had really happened. But people saw it. They were in my dad's twenty-two foot open skiff. It had a sixty-five horse Grey marine. They had to run outside from Stump Pass up to the Venice Jetty. He'd handled boats all his life but he made a miscalculation that time. A squall came out of the west. He was making a run for the jetty, hoping to make it before the high tide change. But when he got off the jetty the tide was beginning to run out, and there was one hell of a chop right off the mouth of the jetty. He should have beached it. He tried to run in and took a wave aboard that swamped the engine. It swung sideways in the chop and broached. It probably clipped my mother when it went over. There were people on the jetty, watching. Apparently he was making no attempt to save himself. They say he kept diving and diving, looking for her, as the tide kept carrying him further and further out. By the time they got out there with boats, he was gone for good. They found her, but they never found him."

"Were there other children?"

"I was the only one."

"What happened to you?"

"I had to move in with a bachelor uncle, a sour-friendless mean son of a bitch. Excuse me."

"That's all right."

"I was a pretty wild kid for a while. I guess I was trying to work my way into Raiford State Prison. But I got serious about football just in time."

"It must be so odd to look at the Gulf and . . . think of that happening."

"In the first few months I used to come over here onto the Key and just sit and look at it. I guess I made it into something with an intelligence of its own. It was evil. It laughed at me. I wanted to go out to the middle of it, halfway to Mexico and dive down and yank out the plug and let the damn thing run down into hell and explode into steam. Then I would find my father. But . . . one day it was just another piece of ocean, as enduring and impersonal as a mountain range. If you get careless it will kill you, just as a mountain will or a forest fire. But there is no intent."

We had arrived back at the towel. She turned to face me in an almost formal way and said, "When you were fumbling around with that silly shell, I didn't know how glad I was going to be that you'd hang around."

"Any time."

"And you haven't acted . . . silly or slimy, and I don't think you could, so I'm glad of that too."

She was smiling. We looked into each other's eyes. And in a fractional part of that moment, the relationship changed to something new. I don't think she was expecting it any more than I was. It is that sudden rapport that goes so much further than words. It is a kind of recognition. In that curious instant, the other person becomes an obligatory part of your future. But even as I saw her smile fade and her mouth soften and her eyes take on a startled look, I wondered if this was the way she had looked at Charlie Haywood.

"I haven't met anybody here," she said.

"Not lately?"

"I don't understand that—the way you say that. Are you angry?"

"Confused, I guess."

"It doesn't take long to get tired of sitting in there and looking at television."

"Year after year?"

"You really aren't married?"

We were entrapped there by each other's eyes. There

84

was a breathlessness in her voice. "I was once."

"I'd go out with you if you'd ask me."

"Why are you so anxious about whether I'm married?"

"Because I don't think it would be smart—if you were."

"But it's okay if you are?"

"I'm not married!"

"You just live with the guy?"

"I live with a gray Persian cat His name is Eerie. That's because he watches things that aren't there."

"I am getting very very confused, Mrs. Weber."

"Good Lord!" she said "Oh, my goodness! I'm Peggy Varden! Char is my sister, my half-sister. And she's nine years older than I am."

The world dropped back into a pattern I could understand. I snapped my fingers. "You come from Richmond?"

"Yes. I got here yesterday. I was here last year for two weeks, but a little earlier in the summer."

"And you're not married?"

"I used to be. When I was a child. Peter died when I was twenty—that was five years ago."

"I'm sorry I got so mixed up."

She tried to glower at me. It was essentially too merry a face to make the expression very effective. "Do you have any distinguishing marks or characteristics? Like a name?"

"I'm handling everything damn well this morning. Sam Brice."

"Sam Brice. Why should it be familiar, sort of?"

"It's familiar, sort of, to only the most hardened addicts of pro football, Peggy. The ones who even learn the names of the linemen."

"Hey!" she said. "Sure. Peter was wild about the game, and I caught the disease from him. He taught me how to watch it. And I still do. But you . . ."

"I'm not around any more."

"Not for the last three seasons, at least."

"Not for exactly the last three seasons."

"Oh, Sam, I remember one fabulous Sunday afternoon you had. Was it the second year you played? Against the Redskins at Washington. I saw that one. You were into their backfield like a tiger."

85

"I was really up for that one. And I was working a special deal with our right guard and the linebacker to get loose. I got mousetrapped a few times, but we'd figured on that. It wasn't until the last quarter they came up with the right way to contain what we'd worked out."

"Why did you quit when you were doing so well?"

"It's a long story."

"Sam. That's a sort of good solid, durable name."

"As in Sam Huff?"

"Do I have to kick you with my bad leg, or come back at you with the big broad hint all over again?"

"What time will I pick you up?"

"Are you going to feed me?"

"Miles and miles from here."

"Like a little after six then?"

"I shall report on time, Margaret."

"It didn't come from Margaret. It just started as Peggy. And I am being shameless because I had just about the dullest vacation of my life last year when I came down here, and I wasn't ever going to come back, except Char wrote such a lonely-sounding letter."

Ack's small car was gone when I walked back to his place. I put on my clothes, put his magpie shell in his mailbox, had breakfast and still got to the office at an average time for the summer months. Alice Jessup and Jennie Benjamin were breaking in a new girl, a temporary replacement, as Jennie explained firmly. The new one was very young, with a hippy rolling walk, a narrow swarthy face and a look of sullen insolence. Her name was Mary May Frear. There are a lot of Frears in the area, and some of them are pretty trashy folk, and I had the feeling this wasn't going to work out.

Bunny Biscoe came in to see me a little after eleven and we went across the street for coffee. When you look at him all you see is a huge nose, jug ears, an underlip stuck out like a shelf, and saucery pale blue eyes. These seem to take up all the room on his small head. His byline is the one that appears most frequently in the *Florence City Ledger*. He is a nice, persevering, stupid little guy who can get some of the simplest news stories so mixed up nobody can ever figure out exactly what happened.

He wanted to pump me about Sis, but I got more out of him than he got out of me. I learned they were now using borrowed helicopters in the hunt for the little black Renault, hoping to spot it on one of the little sandy roads that wind off into the empty land east of the city. T.C. Barley, the state's attorney, was now taking an active interest in the case and more and more police talent was being brought in. A few reporters had come down from Sarasota, Tampa and St. Pete, and up from Fort Myers. Sheriff Pat Millhaus had been taped for a television news program out of Tampa.

The day seemed to drag along. I made an afternoon call in Osprey to appraise the damage on a sideswiped panel delivery truck, then went back to the office and inserted some new price lists on foreign car parts into my work books. By five o'clock I was standing—singing and scrubbing—in the shower when the phone rang.

"Sam? This is Peggy Varden."

"You see, I even have a phone listed in my name."

"I'm terribly sorry, but I have a little headache and I guess I'd better cancel it for tonight." Her tone sounded very flat and formal and unfriendly.

"I could bring aspirin."

"Thank you so much for asking me."

"How about the same time tomorrow night?"

"Oh, my leg feels perfectly all right now, thank you."

"I get it. Sorry to be so slow. If you can sneak out and still want to go out, give me a polite no answer."

"No, I'm sorry. That won't be possible."

"If it has to be later than we planned, give me another no."

"Thank you, but that won't be possible either, Mr. Brice."

"If you can get up the road to meet me on the beach in front of D. Ackley Bush's house say something else about the leg."

"No, I didn't realize a cramp could be so painful."

"I'll do a slow count by half hours starting with six, and when I get to the right one, say goodby and hang up. Six, six-thirty, seven, seven-thirty, eight, eight-thirty, nine, nine-thirty, ten . . ."

"Thank you for asking me anyway. Good-by Sam."

Chapter Six

I WAS IN no mood for conversation with Ack and the inevitable explanations, so I unhooked the chain across the Turner driveway and put my wagon in there, hidden in the black shadows of the tall casuarinas that were sighing in an east wind. I knew they were away until late September, and would have approved if given all the information.

After I had strolled down the beach I was in position at quarter to ten. After the booming thunderstorm at eight o'clock, the sky had cleared and the world smelled new. There was a half-moon silvering the beach, and enough phosphorescence so that I could see the quick streak of a questing fish from time to time. I sat in the moon shadow of a sea grape on a half-buried palm log. I saw her when she was a hundred yards away. She came swinging along in a balanced and rhythmic way that made my heart veer sideways and then steady back on course. When she was closer I stood up and moved into the moonlight. She carried her purse and shoes. She wore a dark strapless top, a full pale skirt.

She marched up to me and said, "I resent being turned into a sneak. I am not a creepy little kid. I am a twenty-five-year-old widow. I'll make my own judgments on people and pick my own friends."

"Whoa! I haven't said a word."

"You better take me to a fun place, Sam, and it better be a late night."

"Don't put your shoes on yet. There's a little more walking."

As I rehooked the chain I decided on a place to go. It meant a fairly long ride, but it gave us a chance to talk. Sometimes you get the feeling that you can never get all the way talked out with one special person.

"They didn't like the idea of your going out?"

"Not one little bit. Just like last year, except last year I didn't even get a chance. They're so damn strange about it. They have the lovely house and the beach and the pool and the servants and the boat, and they don't want to go anywhere—or want anybody else to go. Because I'm a guest, Sam, I couldn't actually blow up. I had to play the whole thing slightly cool. There was all the pressure about going out with somebody I hadn't met in a proper way. And there being nobody in the whole area I could safely go out with, and nowhere to go if I did go out. So I made the call hoping you'd catch on they could hear me. And you did almost too well. You have the talent of a born sneak."

"I notice you got out."

"We're both sneaks. I went into the yawning routine. Just as I figured, they moved from the living room television to their bedroom television after I went to bed. Thank God Charity had briefed me on their burglar alarm system. When any door or window is closed you better not open it again until you cut it off at a handy switch. And then when you close it again, it reactivates the alarm system. I went right out the front door, bold as brass."

"They lead a very quiet life."

"It's a very odd life, Sam. I guess it's what they want. But it seems—unhealthy to me. I couldn't live like that. Few people could."

"Is there any special reason for living like that?"

"I think it's his choice, not hers. But she goes along with it. You see, I don't really know her very well. That must sound strange to you."

"You said she's your half-sister."

"Not even that, actually. Step-sister, but that's such an ugly word. When her father married my mother, she was ten and I was one. I adjusted just fine, but I guess it made her feel like a displaced person. I know she ran

89

away a couple of times, and when she was seventeen she ran away for good. That left me, as an eight-year-old, the eldest of three, and I liked that, so I was secretly glad she was gone. When Daddy finally located her she was married and singing in a club in Reno, and she wouldn't come home and he couldn't make her. She was lovely. She is still a very handsome woman."

"She was married to this Weber?"

"Oh, no! He's her third husband. The first one got a divorce, and I guess it was one of those messy ones, because he got full custody of their baby and she has never seen it since. Then she married a man who owned a night club in Las Vegas. After they were married a year, he was killed. I guess they thought she knew something about it, because they held her for a long time trying to find out from her who had killed her husband and why, but she didn't tell them anything. I guess he left her quite a bit of money. She moved to Chicago and that must have been where she met Maurice. They were married about five years ago, I think, when she was about twenty-eight. I know absolutely nothing about him, except, of course, that he certainly has all the money he seems to need.

"She got in touch with me after they moved down here, about a year after Peter died. I had decided to stay on in Richmond. Peter and I had been happy there. You like places where you have been happy, even after the happiness stops. Peter's uncle had given me a good job. There didn't seem to be very much point in going back home to Dayton. I don't know how she got my address, but she wrote to me saying she didn't want to correspond with her father and please not to tell him where she was living. I . . . just got into the habit of corresponding with her. Last summer I came down, as I told you. It was weird. Never again, I told myself. And here I am again, just because, dammit, she sounded so crushed when I tried to beg off."

"Glad you could make it," I told her.

She hitched closer to me. "I think I am too, Sam."

She told me about Peter Varden, about how they had married when they were too young—just seventeen and nineteen. Her people and Peter's uncle had helped them out, so he could get his degree from Duke. By carrying a heavy work load he had graduated a month before turning twenty-one. He had gone into an insurance office in Richmond. He was doing quite well. When she was four months' pregnant and they were in the midst of house hunting, they said he had fallen in the office and had been taken to the hospital. She learned he had slipped on a freshly waxed tile floor and hit his head on the corner of a desk. The blow had not fractured his skull, but it had ripped a vein. They operated to relieve the pressure of the hemorrhage. He had regained consciousness after the operation, but had gone quickly into coma and had lived a little over a week and then died.

"I was a mess, Sam. I just couldn't cope. I went back to Dayton and lost the baby there, and I went right down to skin and bones. If somebody asked me what time it was, I'd burst into tears. If there was a sudden noise, I'd jump seven feet, screaming. It seemed like such a damn foolish way for a man like that to die.

"One day something changed inside me. As if something went click. I hadn't been able to sleep, but suddenly I was able to go to bed and sleep. Lord, how I slept! Twenty hours at a stretch, take a long walk, eat like a lion and go right back to bed. I guess I had realized I had to go on living, finally. So I went back to Richmond. I went to work for John Pennwalter, Peter's uncle. He has four expensive dress shops. Now I'm assistant manager of one of them. I work in all four, though. I do some modeling, and buy a lot of the sports wear for all four shops, plan sales and ads and write some copy. There's always enough to do."

"It sounds like a good thing for you to be doing, I guess."

"In a sense, yes. But I don't want to do it forever. The situation of being a widow hasn't been the easiest thing in the world, Sam."

"How come?"

"It was pretty sickening in the beginning. We'd had good friends, and the real good ones handled it just right, and they're still friends. But some of the others! Ugh! I don't have any illusions about myself, Sam. I'm better looking than the average gal. By nature I'm sort of frank

and open and friendly, and too many times men seem
to think that my manner is some kind of a sexual approach. The slimy ones gathered around after I went
back to Richmond. They were married, of course. They
put it in a lot of vague and fancy ways, but the general
idea was that I'd turn into a nervous wreck if I was
suddenly deprived of the privilege of going to bed with
somebody, and they would be glad to take care of things,
in a very discreet way. Damn it, I am a very moral kind
of person. I resent being taken for a slut. And some
friends suddenly stopped being friends. After the third
or fourth mealy proposition I invented the right answer,
'Sure,' I would say. 'Thanks a lot for thinking of me.
But let's bring your little wife into this while it's still in
the planning phase, so we won't run into any conflict of
schedules. One of us will take Monday, Wednesday and
Friday and the other Tuesday, Thursday and Saturday,
and we'll all take Sunday off. Why don't I phone her
right now? I'm telling you, Sam, they look at you with
what I guess is called mixed emotions.'"

I laughed and she joined me. It felt good to laugh that
way, riding north through the night, laughing with a
lovely girl.

"Your turn, Sam," she said. "You were married once,
you said."

"But she took off. She's married to somebody else."

I wanted to tell it to Peggy more carefully than I had
told it to other people. We went up through Sarasota
and across the Ringling Bridges and out Longboat Key
to the Colony Beach Club. I parked and we walked
around by the pool and into the big bar lounge and on
to the second room where Charlie Davies was playing
a gentle and skillful and romantic piano for two couples
dancing slowly in the shadows, and a half-dozen other
people at the tables. It had been almost a year since I
had seen Charlie. This was the slow pace of summer,
pleasant, nostalgic.

I took Peggy back to a table near the window wall that
fronts on the Gulf beach. The wind had shifted enough
to put a small curl of surf on that beach, sparkling with
phosphorescence. The cocoanut palms were floodlighted.
We settled for a pair of tall rum collins. Rum is a good

summer drink. Charlie moved into *I'll Be Seeing You.*

"Golly!" my girl said.

"Like it?"

"You certainly pick a mood place, my large friend, ol' Sam."

Yes, I'd picked a mood place. And I remembered that I had been going to bring Sis to this same place, long ago, and somehow we'd never made it.

The pang of guilt was sharp as a blade.

I knew I had no right in the world to be having as good a time as I was by merely being with this Peggy girl. But I did not see how I could turn it all off. Selfishness is sometimes totally inadvertent. Even as I felt guilt and a kind of shame about being able to have thrust Sis out of my mind, I knew it was going to happen again, and I would feel the same guilt again, and it would keep on like that for just as long as the situation continued. This girl had a magic talent for gaiety.

"Something wrong?" she asked suddenly.

"No. Why?"

"You were way off somewhere, and I had the feeling you didn't like it there."

"I didn't. I better come right back here. I like it here."

(Goodby, Sis, for a little while. You would be the very first to understand that it isn't disloyalty to you, or callousness. It's bewitchment.)

By unspoken consent we dropped the personal history bit and lived in the present. And it was a very good present to be in if you want a good place to start something fresh and new. We talked nonsense. We danced a few times and she followed my cumbersome lead so well she made me feel as if I knew how. Charlie Davies came over to the table between sets and I introduced him and told him I had lowered my standards to the extent that I was now escorting tourist women to low dives. She told him she was paying me a dollar a day for the escort service and was beginning to feel cheated. Charlie and I talked of some of the old places where I had heard his piano, the Sarabar, the Dolphin, the Elbow Room. He said I was staying away so long these days he was afraid he'd forget my name. Peggy told him she had some plans that would get me back maybe every night for a while. When he asked her what she'd like to hear, she named good ones. Later, after we had become the only customers left, we went and sat at the stools at the showbar piano, and had that one for the road while Charlie sang the late, late ballads. Peggy knew how to listen, and she liked the right things.

We went back to an all night restaurant in town, for steak and french fries, and some black coffee to take the impact off the rum. And somehow it was once again time to go into history when she reminded me of where my personal saga had been interrupted.

"She sounds like a brat," Peggy said.

"It wasn't that. She just couldn't live the way she would have had to live."

"Then she didn't love you."

"She thought she did. She believed she did. So maybe that is as good as the real thing—or as close as she could get to love."

"But there's one thing I don't understand, Sam."

I could sense it coming, but I said, "What?"

"Couldn't you have just . . . stayed in pro ball?"

"For the money and the happy marriage. I was thrown out of pro ball, Peggy."

She looked very startled. "Why?"

"They didn't feel they could trust me."

She frowned. "I don't understand."

I sighed. "Here it is, then. A game with the Browns was coming up in Cleveland. She always went on road trips. But we had a hell of a battle about nothing at all, so she didn't go. On Saturday night I left the hotel in Cleveland and went bar hopping, feeling sore and reckless. Somewhere during the evening, after things got dim, I found myself at a table with two strangers and I was arguing the point that any one man on a team could throw a game, provided it was a close enough game. Suddenly I got slipped three hundred bucks, three one hundred dollar bills under the table. A great light dawned. I rolled them up into a little ball between my palms and dropped them into the nearest drink and asked them if they wanted to go outside and discuss it. They didn't want to. So I left. We won the next day. The hangover didn't affect my play. I don't think I thought once of those two guys. A week later I found myself summoned to Mr. Bert Bell's office. There I identified pictures of the two guys who had propositioned me. I didn't know they had followed me from the hotel, waiting until I was well along before moving in on me. And they didn't know they were being followed by two ex-FBI men who watched the whole deal. There were lawyers there too. It was all explained carefully to me. I had agreed to report any such attempt. Not only hadn't I reported it formally, I had not told any of the guys about it. I still don't know why. Keeping the pro game clean is a great responsibility. I could no longer be trusted. I could not prove that I was not just hanging back waiting for a better offer. I had protected those men by not reporting them. The season was nearly over. I'd be paid for the full season. But stay away from the squad, Brice. And no contract next year. Try to fight it, and you'll only hurt the game and accomplish nothing. Bell shook my hand. He felt sorry about the whole thing. So did I, but that's the way it was. I suppose they were right. But I could never have . . . sold out to anybody."

She was quick to reach across the narrow table and place her hand on mine. "I'm sorry, Sam. I'm very sorry. I'm sorry most of all that it still hurts, doesn't it?"

"I tell myself it doesn't, but I guess it always will. They shouldn't smash you so completely for one little hunk of stupidity. But what else could they do?"

"What else indeed? Can't you think of at least ten men who would have gotten off with a reprimand?"

"I don't think about that, Peggy."

"One passing quarterback who can fake well and run when he has to, is worth how many defensive tackles?"

"Get off that bit, Peggy."

"I'm sorry. It just makes me mad, that's all."

"I tell myself that a grown man should not be concerned about a game which is concerned with moving an oblong leather inflated object from one end to the other of a pasture one hundred yards long."

"It is as valid as the things most men concern themselves with."

"It's a ball game, and the hell with it."

So we got back into the car and rolled south toward

95

Friday morning. I parked again in Turner's drive.

"Now we walk for our health," she said. We walked north, after hiding her purse and shoes between the roots of a pine. We walked all the way to Orange Beach, and sat on a cement picnic bench. She had seemed subdued during the walk.

"What time is it, Sam?"

"Twenty after four."

"In a little while we can start feeling virtuous about being up so early. Won't that be nice?"

"I can hardly wait."

She turned toward me. "Sam, I am cursed with a logical mind. It's something no woman should have. And so I have to ask you a question."

"Like what?"

"You went through that laborious routine with the shell this morning. You came sidling up like a bison on tiptoe."

"I'm a very deft guy."

"But you thought I was Charity. So right from the beginning, when you were plotting the shell routine, you thought I was Charity."

"And if I did?"

"She does swim there often in the early morning. And she does collect shells. So, with her, the shell thing might have been more effective."

"Probably."

"Were you trying to set up some kind of romance, Sam?"

"What would you think of such a project?"

"I think it would be damn dirty."

"In what way?"

"You would have heard she's . . . well, she's a dish, I guess. And, because of the way he likes to live, probably bored and lonely."

"I've seen her, but from quite a distance. Nice build."

"So it's summer and you haven't got anything better to do, so why not try to take a hack at the vulnerable wife of the rich recluse. He's better than twenty years older than she is. And it might have worked."

"But it turned out to be you."

"Sam, I don't want to think you capable of that sort of—sly attempt at adventure."

"So, because you are a bright girl and you do have a logical mind, you probably have some kind of a second guess."

"The man who tried to rob their safe is loose. Newspaper people have been trying to bother them. Anna told me about the police tramping all over the place Tuesday, the day before I arrived. A silly little man stands guard all night."

"I'd forgotten about LeRoy."

"He had some wise words of warning about how I shouldn't be wandering around in the night, not with a criminal loose in the area. I thanked him and told him he was doing a splendid job, and just keep on guarding like crazy. Anyway, a girl is missing too. My darn logical mind has been hopping back and forth between the idea that you were making a play for Char, and the idea you wanted to just strike up a conversation and ask her some things, maybe."

"Which would you like it to be?"

"Don't tease me, Sam."

"Do you love your step-sister?"

"I guess I feel a certain loyalty to her. But we haven't got very much in common. She's quite strange. I don't know."

"Have you got time to listen to a long story?"

"I have to be back to work in two weeks."

I hesitated, thinking of the ways I should edit the account, shift the emphasis, spare her some of my more lurid guesses. But with a mental shrug I decided she would have it cold and straight.

I talked the world gray, and talked the first edge of the sun up.

Then I waited for comment. She looked at me solemnly. "Do you love that Gantry girl?"

"You are a dandy. Of all the things you could have said. . . . You know, that's quite a departure for a girl with a logical mind. What's more, it's very revealing, in a flattering way."

Her blush was as pretty as the warm morning. "Darn you, stop hedging."

"I liked Sis. I still do. I needed her. I got over needing

97

her. It wasn't anything anybody has to be ashamed of. You would like her too."

She shivered "It's all so dark and creepy and strange, all of it. I don't know what to think. Sam, I would feel better if you sort of kissed me. Not in an important way or anything. Just for close."

And so I did. It was a special sweetness. It soon showed all the signs of becoming very important indeed, and so with simultaneous impulse, we ended it.

"I've known you at least ten years," she said. "It's so odd."

"We have a twenty-four hour anniversary coming up."

She held my wrist tightly. "Maybe you've sort of built the whole thing up out of nothing. I mean maybe Maurice and Charity are just . . . what they seem."

"He was seeing her . . . Charlie Haywood was."

"Which must have taken some very tricky planning."

"She let him go to prison. He could have gotten the schedule from her. She couldn't know about the boat breaking down. He was doing something she had talked him into doing. He took that risk for her."

"She seems very nervous and restless, much more so than last year."

"During the two weeks you were here last year, did Weber ever mention his background?"

"Never."

"That's too damn odd to be real, Peggy."

"What's in that safe?"

"Money, probably. So Charlie and Charity could run off together."

"But she lives so well. And that has always been important to her. The luxuries. Servants, a big house."

"You're sensitive to the way people feel. What's the relationship between those two, Peggy?"

"Well . . . they're very quiet and sort of polite to each other. But . . . maybe I'm imagining it, but it's like the way people would have to be if they were on an island and knew they couldn't get off. Do you know what I mean?"

"I think so."

"You have to adapt to something that exists, I guess,

98

or wear yourself out fighting it. He's in charge, Sam. There's no question about that. She seems to wait for some clue from him before going ahead with anything, and she has a sort of anxiety about pleasi . . . no, not pleasing him . . . about not crossing him."

"Any affection at all?"

"None! Not a smidgen. And no love either. But . . . pretty strong and pretty obvious in the sex bracket. I have the feeling it isn't as hefty this year as last year, Sam, but I haven't been here very long. He's a very . . . I don't know how to say it. An animal kind of a man. And it's always at his option. It made me feel quite strange last year. It could be morning, afternoon or evening, and he would get a kind of lowering look, and pretty soon there'd be some word or gesture and off she would go with him, meek and humble and obedient. But it was all done in such a cold way."

"And no clue to his background?"

"I think he's quite an ignorant man, Sam. He has very little to say. When he forgets himself, his grammar is poor. He opens doors and things like that, but his table manners are frightful, really. He gobbles. Everything is gone in a minute. He has no . . . air of importance. I don't know how to say it. I don't want to sound like a snob. But he's like a man who came to fix the drains and happened to move in and take over somehow."

"What's she like?"

Peggy shrugged. "I guess she's seen and done everything there is. And some of it was nasty. From forty feet away, in her swim suit, baking beside the pool, she looks like a show girl. She knows how to walk and sit and stand. Sometimes, in a sort of frenzy, she fights that pool until she is almost too exhausted to climb out of it. She spends hours on her face and figure, nails and hair. When she talks she has too much fake animation in her face . . . a lot of business with the eyebrows . . . which is the show biz syndrome, I guess. I don't know whether she strained her voice singing or whether whiskey did the trick, but it's a kind of baritone whisper if you can imagine that. When you see her face close up, even when she's using that forced animation, you suddenly realize it's the most exhausted face in the whole world. Her eyes have been dead for a thousand years. Her teeth are capped. I don't know why I came back here. My family has the vacation address. But they don't know who she really is."

"Much drinking?"

"He takes it easy. She starts about four o'clock and builds, so she's quietly bagged come bedtime. But never sloppy drunk. Just very remote."

"Does she ever go out alone in that convertible?"

"What convertible? There's only one car, that four-year-old Continental. It hasn't got much mileage on it, though."

"That's the way I think she met Charles Haywood, when they went to Mel Fifer's agency and bought a convertible for cash. Charlie was a salesman there. And maybe that gave her the freedom of action so she could meet him."

"I guess it was sold. There's only the one car. What would she do with a car? She never goes anywhere."

"Not any more. How about the servants?"

"Three very nice, quiet, inconspicuous people. Stan Chase has all the instincts of a hermit. He coddles the Sea Queen as if he owned it. The Mahlers tend strictly to business, and they keep the relationship sort of . . . formal, but they are kindly people, I think."

The sun had hoisted itself high enough to bring customers to the public beach. They stared at us with open curiosity.

"Let's hike back," she said, and yawned.

After a silent few minutes she said, "Sam?"

"Yes, honey."

"Mmm. Unplanned term of endearment. Sam, I know what you want to ask and I can guess why you think you shouldn't ask it of me."

"Yes?"

"But I'll do it anyway. I'll be the girl spy, dauntless adventuress. And report to you, sir."

"There may be nothing to find out."

"There's *something* to find out. And maybe it won't have anything at all to do with that Charlie or your Sis friend . . ."

"You snarl when you mention her."

"Simple, inexplicable jealousy. Be flattered."

"I'm flattered."

"You're even smug. As I was saying, it may not solve your mystery, but maybe I can solve the mystery of Maurice and Charity. The more I think about them, the more strange they seem."

"Without sounding like your maiden aunt, Peggy, please be damn careful. Meddling got one person a five year jail term. Whatever he doesn't want found out, he's taking a lot of pains and money to protect. I don't think it would be a healthy thing to have him find out you're prying."

She smiled up at me. "Thank you, Auntie." And it did seem a little absurd in that reassuring warmth of the early sun.

"She's been mixed up with the law."

"A long time ago."

"They're both hiding from something, and they don't want to be found."

"Pure assumption."

"Play it like dangerous, Peggy. Will you do that?"

"Sure. I like the protective bit. I like you, Sam. I like you one hell of a lot. Will you keep that in mind?"

"Permanently."

"I am not a vacationing cupcake looking for a fast romp with no boring complications."

"You didn't have to say that, you know."

"When I'm clarifying my own attitude, you hush up."

"Yes ma'am."

"This was the best evening I've had in this last fifth of my life, Sam."

"It's been hard to find this kind any more."

"Since Sis?"

"For God's sake!"

She laughed at me. "I can make you look like a wounded moose. That gives me a sense of power. When do I sneak out and meet you again?"

"Tonight?"

"When else? Same time, same place, same girl."

I checked where we were. "Two miles shouldn't be that short," I said. "We've walked past the shoes and purse."

101

"It's all autohypnosis. I've read about it."

We went back and picked up her stuff. As she straightened up she said, "Left one thing out, didn't you?"

"Probably. But what?"

"Yesterday morning, when you stared at me in that strange way. It's because I look like Judy?"

"How would you know that?"

"Nothing else could have made you react that way. Do I look too much like her?"

"What would be too much?"

"Where you wouldn't really be seeing me. You'd be seeing a ghost."

"No. I see you now. The face is different. The hair is different."

"Something else is different, Sam."

"What's that?"

"The heart is different. I am a steady girl. I have the constant heart. You should run like a rabbit, Sam. When I make a commitment, all the cards go face up, and facing you. So if you have been trying to be a different person all night, trying to fit yourself to me, and you are not at all what you have been pretending to be, then you had best run. I mean it."

"I think this is what I am, Peggy. Does anybody ever really know?"

"I can play ten thousand little games, but no big games. Am I alarming you?"

No eyes could be steadier than those of a green such as I had never seen before. The left one was set a half-millimeter higher than the right one, and the left brow had a slightly higher arch.

Without taking my eyes from hers, I said, "The eyelashes are like dark copper, but the eyebrows are darker."

"I cheat with the eyebrows. With a pencil thing. I build up the upper lip with lipstick. I have two moles at the small of my back. I get very messy head colds. I've been known to throw things in anger."

"I'm not alarmed, Peggy."

She stepped back close to the tree, lifted her arms and said, "Let's try this one for importance, Brice." She dropped the purse, the shoes.

102

It was important. Perhaps a kiss—which is objectively a ludicrous thing, a joining of mouths—is a special form of interrogation and response. We told each other that this could never be a trivial thing. It could be a lot of things, tender, strong, savage and sweet. But never trivial.

The sound of the car heading north on Orange Road broke it up. I saw Luxey go by at the wheel of a county car.

"That's the polite little man who didn't want me to wander around in the dark," she said.

"That's the polite little man who collapsed me with a night stick."

"That one?"

"A viper is a very small thing. So is a scorpion. So is a flu germ." I picked up the purse and shoes.

"Thank you. I'm drunk on morning air and no sleep and being kissed, Sam."

"It's a good way to be."

I walked her to the strip of Weber beach. A deeply tanned woman came down the narrow path through the sea oats. She wore a vivid yellow swim suit with a small skirt effect, and carried a matching beach bag. She was handsomely built, and I knew at once that this was the floozy hair Gus had seen in Charlie's car. It was worn long, and it was as spurious as a new dime, lifeless as the flax on a store window dummy.

She registered shock and said to Peggy, in an aspirated croak, "I thought you were in bed asleep!" She seemed to be aware only of Peggy, but I could see the physical response to me, an arching of the back, a graceful hip-shot stance, shoulders squared to lift the breasts, belly pulled flat.

"Char, may I present Sam Brice. Sam, this is my sister, Charity Weber."

Charity managed a dim smile to go with a look like that of a butcher about to grade and disjoint a side of beef. "How do," she said. "Peggy, why are you dressed like that? When did you go out?"

"Last night, dear. Somewhere around ten. And I happened to run into Sam."

"Where have you been?"

103

"Leading a gay, mad, dancing life, Char."

The woman stared at her. I saw that the deep tan masked some of the corrosion of that face. "Are you drunk, darling?" she asked.

"Just happy. Char, I was going to sneak in and then sneak out again tonight to date Sam again, but now I don't have to sneak any more, do I?"

Mrs. Weber was in an awkward spot. "Maurice says we have . . . . uh . . . . a responsibility to you, dear, so long as you're our house guest. I don't think he'll approve of this. I don't think he'll like it at all."

"What a shame!" Peggy said. "I'll have to take the rest of my vacation in a local motel. I couldn't upset Maurice."

"You know you're welcome to stay with us, darling."

"And go out with Sam. I want that understood, Char."

Charity Weber wheeled on me, and suddenly she had everything working for her, the eyes, the mouth, the figure, all of it aggressive, provocative, flirtatious and ironic. I could see how that practised impact would have blinded Charlie Haywood to the difference in their ages, to the fact of her marriage. Innocent Charlie had been a mouse sandwich for a panther. For the sake of all that humid promise he would have marched woodenly off to pillage Fort Knox.

"You are a big beastie, Sam Brice," she croaked.

"It keeps me out of sports cars."

"Local, aren't you, Sam?" she asked.

"Incurably, Mrs. Weber. I went out into the wide world but they didn't appreciate me out there, and so I came home."

"I compliment your taste, Big Sam. This lovely little sister of mine is a rare kind of creature. Do you sense that?"

"From the first."

"And I have so few house guests, Sam." She moved closer to me. "I do want to enjoy her while she's here. I guess it's only normal she should have the occasional date. You won't be greedy will you?"

"I work for my living, Mrs. Weber."

"I can spare her in the evening, Sam, but if you keep her out all night she'll sleep all day."

104

"It makes me feel strange to have you two splitting me up," Peggy complained.

"I'll be more conservative next time," I said.

"You can come and call for me properly," Peggy said.

"Just stop in front, Sam," Charity said. "You don't have to come to the door. I know it's rude, but Mr. Weber doesn't like callers. People upset him. He's a very shy man. That's why we aren't . . . very social people." She patted my arm quickly. "I think you're going to be very nice about the whole thing, aren't you?"

"Intensely cooperative," I said.

She gave me a somewhat dubious look, then smiled and said, "You children say good night or good morning or whatever it is, while I swim."

She tucked her hair into a yellow cap and walked into the immature surf.

"More cooperative than I expected," Peggy said. "But what else could she do?"

"What else indeed, after that motel remark?"

"I guess that was rude. But I'm not their ward, and I'm not a child. Sam . . . darling. Is that as good to hear as it is to say?"

"Better."

"Darling, I'll solve your mystery for you. I'll be an expert sneak."

"A careful sneak, please. The broad in the yellow suit is a very hard piece of material, Peggy."

"There's something so lost about her."

"And Mikoyan is probably a very disturbed man. But I wouldn't try to hold his hand."

"There's nothing sinister about Char!"

"She didn't mean any harm when she destroyed Charlie Haywood's life. She just did it for the hell of it."

"Go home to bed, Sam. You're getting grouchy."

I walked to the road with her, and walked down the road past Ack's to my parked car. When I looked back she was still standing there, waiting for me to look back, so she could wave.

Chapter Seven

THE ALARM woke me up at two o'clock on Friday afternoon, and I was in the office by three. I took care of some
appraisal reports. No matter what I was doing, Peggy
Varden hovered pleasantly over one corner of my mind.
Nothing she had been able to tell me about the Webers
had been of any help. I wondered if there might be some
helpful information on file over at the County Courthouse, some clues in the papers pertaining to the real
estate transfer, possibly on the photostat of the recorded
deed.

Vince Avery gave me the information on how to find
it in the deed books, referring to the government lot line
number. I went to the office of the County Clerk in the
new wing of the courthouse. I found the photostat of the
deed. The previous owner of record was Mr. Jason Hall of
Tampa. He had sold that particular piece of property to
the Starr Development Company, an Illinois corporation
with the address given as a box number in Chicago. The
necessary documents had been signed by a Mr. E. D.
Dennison, treasurer of the company. I suddenly remembered that Dennison was the name of the man who had
arranged the purchase of the land and the construction of
the house.

I arrived at the office of the County Tax Collector at
five minutes of five. There I learned that the annual
property tax bill, amounting to a little over fourteen hundred dollars, was sent each year to the Starr Development
Company and was paid promptly by cashier's check.

I drove back to my cottage, trying to make sense out of

what I had learned. It was commonly believed that Weber owned the house and land. He could still own it, less directly, if he owned Starr Development. There might be some tax reason for having a corporation own the house. But, between Ack and Peggy, I was beginning to get a picture of a man who would not be likely to own a corporation.

At least I had some new information, but I didn't have any idea what to do with it. By the time I had carried a tall drink out onto my small porch I remembered Lou Leeman. He was one of the very, very few who made a human response when I got into the trouble that wrecked my career. He was on the sports desk at the *Chicago Daily Mirror*. When the rumor spread through the Thump and Sprawl Industry, a lot of people heckled me for a statement. The rumors were so much worse than the actuality I wished I could tell them. But I had given my word.

It was Lou who came up to me in an airport terminal and said, "They tell me you won't talk, Sam."

"They tell you true."

"Out like permanent?"

"Forever and ninety-nine years. My idea, you know. I got sick of the game."

He squared himself away and cocked a smoky blue jaw. "I've watched you too long and too hard, boy. You never dog it. You've never been cute. It's like a laboratory demonstration of a kind of character that has to run all the way through a man. So whatever it was, I would say you're taking a fall for stupidity, not crookedness."

"I just happened to give up the game, Lou."

"If you ever can talk, and . . . if there was anything to talk about . . . who would you come see?"

"Some creep name of Leeman."

I thought about Lou through half a drink, then went in and placed a person to person call. A cooperative long distance operator tracked him down at home.

"A voice from braver days," he said. "Back when the world was young."

"Does this long white beard muffle my voice too much, for God's sake?"

107

"I guess maybe it's blubber. What do you scale, Sam? Three hundred?"

"Two seventeen last time I checked it. Lou, you're the only guy in Chicago who would do me a favor. But I want you to bill me for your time and expenses."

"All I'll ask for is a free-load vacation in Florida."

"It's a deal!" I told him to check out the Starr Development Company and one E. D. Dennison, treasurer of same. I gave him the post-office box number. He told me to wait while he looked in the phone book.

"No Starr Development and no E. D. Dennison listed, pal. Can you clue me on what I'm looking for?"

"I don't know, exactly. I want to find out if it's legitimate or crooked or what the hell it is."

"But it is an Illinois corporation?"

"Yes."

"Then I know where to start. Right at the capitol, at the Attorney General's office, I got a good contact there."

"When can you get on it?"

"Not until Monday morning now. Too late?"

"No. But as soon as you know a thing, Lou, phone me collect." I gave him both phone numbers. We chatted a little while longer about other things, and then I went back to my half-drink.

At nine o'clock I stopped the wagon on the road in front of the Weber place. I could see lights through the plantings, but I could not see the house. I gave one genteel beep on the horn. Peggy did not exactly come out at a dead run, but she wasted no time. Yet, just as I started to open the car door on my side to go around and open the door for her, a familiar light blinded me.

"You again," LeRoy said in a disgusted voice.

"Which part of my head do you want to beat?"

"Smart talk me, mister, and I'll whip all parts of it up down and around. What you want around here?"

"He came to pick me up," Peggy said in a flat and deadly tone of voice. "And he may do it quite often." The light swiveled and steadied on her for a moment and then clicked out.

"I got to check anything that moves around here in the night time," Luxey said stubbornly. "If'n he stops here forty times a night he gets checked out every time. That's the orders I got given to me, ma'am. And you worried me all the night through last night, ma'am, the way you went wandering off onto the beach and never did come back. I didn't know as I should tell anybody because it didn't come under guarding the place. When I come on tonight I looked in a window and seen you and felt better."

"Darn it, that's so sweet I can't stay mad at you. But I am mad at you for hitting Mr. Brice on the head, officer."

"You call me Depity. Depity LeRoy Luxey, ma'am. If'n this Brice weren't so big he wouldn't got hit so fast, but the size I am, I can't stand around on one laig talking polite to a smart-mouth man in the dark what won't answer questions sensible and comes at me. Frankly, I don't care if he's got hard feelings or not, but I just as soon you wouldn't, ma'am, being as how you could understand how it is."

"I got smacked for being stupid, Luxey. And that's the story of my life."

"From now on blank your lights on and off twice and I won't bother you none," he said, and he faded silently off into the shadows.

I started up as soon as Peggy was beside me. "Find a dark place and whoa this thing, Sam," she said.

I pulled off to the left under the pines beyond the Turner place, and killed the lights. As I turned toward her, she dug herself into my arms and laced her small fingers together at the nape of my neck. "How's this for restraint?" she asked with laughter behind her voice. "How's this for demure and shy?"

"I've got to admit it's efficient."

After a miraculous darkness of long minutes she plumped back to her side of the seat with a great sigh of satisfaction. "Drive on," she said. "I had to make sure I hadn't imagined the whole thing. Where are we going?"

"I thought I'd ask you to name the kind of place and I'll find it."

"Sam?"

"Yes, honey."

"Sam, you know I haven't made my mind up or anything about you."

"I know. But you will."

"One way or the other. Sam?"

"I'm still right here, driving this car, ma'am."

"You remember what I told you . . . about how I'm really a very moral kind of person, but people get the wrong idea?"

"I remember."

"I want to see where you live." She said it defiantly.

I had to laugh at her. She didn't want any misunderstanding.

"Stop braying, dammit," she said.

"Peggy, my friend, I try not to spoil anything that's worth anything. I was going to go through the same routine, only I was going to do it later in the evening, because I'd like you to see the place. I was even going to bring up the moral person bit, so you wouldn't figure it for a fancy pass."

We went to the cottage. "Can I prowl?" she asked, "or do I have to be polite?"

"Prowl, please."

She went through the place like an auditor. The only thing she didn't do was open the bureau drawers. She was like a pet cat in a new house. She wore a cinnamon blouse, a pale gray skirt, sandals. I made drinks, put a background record on, took the drinks out onto the porch and settled down patiently. She turned the living room light out, on her way out, leaving on the one lamp near the window so that there was a faint light on the porch.

She sat and took a sip of her drink and said, "You alarm me."

"I've tried not to."

"You're so darn tidy. I live amid piles of junk. Nice clean junk, but piles of it. And there's more books and records than I would have guessed."

"Cultural pretention. To impress girls."

"Hmmm. No pictures of Judy?"

"Why should there be? Why should I salt a wound?"

"Or of Sis?"

"That would have the flavor of a trophy, and that wasn't the way it was."

"Do you mind the prying, Sam? Does it bother you?"

"In anybody else in the world it would. But I have the feeling it's something you had to do."

110

"I wouldn't do it to anybody else in the world. I have better manners. I think we'd better yank the conversation out of this whole general area. Time for my report, sir."

"I knew you'd found out something, or you wouldn't have saved it."

"I think I must be getting too darn obvious or something. Anyhow, I don't think it's much. I flew into Tampa two days ago, on Wednesday, the seventeenth. I flew Eastern down, same as last time. They met me last year at Tampa International. She said they'd meet me again this year. But it was Herman who met me. He said Char had a headache and Maurice was too busy. I don't know what he'd be so darn busy about. Herman has very little conversation, so it was a dull ride down from Tampa. By the time I arrived, Charity was about three drinks along, but she still looked tired. There is a guest wing with a suite. I turned it down last time. It seemed too grand. It wasn't even offered to me this time. I got the same room as before, in the main part of the house. And the darn room smelled like cigars. The air conditioning was on, but it still smelled like stale cigars. I didn't think much about it at the time. I thought Maurice had been in there for some reason. He smokes cigars. Is this getting too involved?"

"Not yet."

She took something from the pocket of her skirt and handed it to me. I could tell by the feel that it was a packet of book matches. I looked at it by the flame of my lighter. The matches were from a bar on Burgundy Street in the Quarter in New Orleans.

"I found them on the floor of my closet," she said proudly.

"Proving what?"

"Anna Mahler is a demon housekeeper. She sticks to a schedule. Saturdays she mops and dusts, closets and all. She'd no more miss those matches than she'd miss a dead horse. Cigar smell, plus matches, plus her iron schedule means recent guests."

"It maybe means something worth checking."

"That's what I thought, so I did. I nailed Anna in the kitchen when she was starting to fix dinner. I scrounged a snack and hung around and engaged her in idle talk, steering it around to the idea that with a house so big she had a lot of work to do, and if there were guests all the time it would be too much for one woman and so on. Finally there was a breakthrough. Two men arrived after dark on the twelfth, just one week ago tonight. They arrived late and Mr. Weber must have known they were coming because he had stayed up, apparently waiting for them, but he hadn't warned Anna, and she was a little bit miffed at that. They stayed four days, and left after dark on Tuesday. They had a rental car. They had never stayed there before. And Charity was sick all the time they were there. She had her meals served in her room."

"It's . . . very interesting, Peggy."

"I got just a little bit too inquisitive, and she suddenly closed right up again, so I went wandering off with an air of great indifference. But if your key night is last Monday night, there were a pair of strange men in the house."

"Names or descriptions?"

"No names. And the only wisp of description is Anna's statement that they were 'city men', whatever that may mean. And I had the feeling, Sam, that when she suddenly clammed up, she'd been given the impression . . . not an order . . . not to talk about any house guests they might have."

"It's a damn queer household."

She was curled up in the big chair, her face in shadow except where the edge of the light touched the jeweled gleam of one eye.

"Up until today," she said in a thoughtful tone, "I thought it was just sort of odd and stuffy and . . . ingrown. Now it's getting sinister, sort of. I don't really know her at all. I can sense that he feels that letting me come to visit her is . . . a special concession. I did just a little bit more prying after I talked to Anna."

"You'll have to be . . ."

"Careful. Yes. I sense that more and more, Sam. Char and I were in the living room waiting for Anna to say dinner was ready. Maurice was somewhere else in the house. So I just kept trying to establish a conversation that would make it logical for her to tell me about having guests who left just before I arrived, and logical for her

112

to mention being sick while they were there. It wasn't a direct kind of prying. But it gave her all the chance in the world to mention it. And she didn't. So she had a good reason not to mention it. She was the one doing the prying. She kept asking me about you. I edited you down to a big, amiable, harmless tower of muscle."

"That's too accurate."

"It is *not!* Anyway, the heat sort of died away. So, at dinner, I brought up Sis Gantry."

"That's a brilliant move! How the hell do you . . ."

"It would have been more obvious *not* to bring it up, Sam. We saw the six o'clock news on channel 13 out of Tampa where they rebroadcast a tape interview with Sheriff Millhaus. He was very cautious. He said that they had no actual evidence to link her disappearance with the information that Charles Haywood had been in the area at the time she disappeared, but they had not discounted the possibility the two things might be connected. After all, it *is* big local news, and, as a house guest, I'd have to talk about it, especially with that fierce little man guarding the house at night. They had already explained about him, you know."

"What did they say?"

"That was the evening of the day I arrived. Charity did the talking. Maurice was there. She just said that a man had broken into the house over two years ago and they'd come home and surprised him, and it had been very upsetting. Now he had escaped from a road gang and had been seen in the area, so a guard had been posted in case he tried to come back, to attempt to rob them again or get even with them for capturing him and turning him in. She said I shouldn't be upset because neither of them thought he would come to the house. It was all . . . just a little too calm and casual."

"So how did you bring Sis into it tonight?"

"I just asked them if they thought Charlie and Sis had gotten together somehow. Maurice just shrugged and kept gobbling his dinner. Charity asked me what I meant. I said that maybe it was a romance and he had escaped to come back to see her, and they had gone off together and that was why she hadn't gotten in touch with anybody because she didn't want to endanger him."

"I think some people have that theory—people who don't know either of them personally."

"Char said it was a marvelous theory. She got practically manic about it, all hopped up about it. She said she had the hunch that that was exactly what happened. Then she said she wished them luck. She hoped they'd get clean away and start a new life together somewhere else and nobody would ever find them again. So I said that was pretty hard to do. Char said it wasn't hard to do if you planned it carefully. Maurice stood up and told her she was a sloppy drunk with a big mouth. He walked away. I'd never heard him say anything like that to her. I'm telling you, it left one big hole in the conversation. Char sat with her eyes shut for a few seconds, and then she opened them and got terribly chatty and vivacious about a lot of trivial nonsense, but all the time she was acting like an actress on a Mike Wallace interview, the tears kept running right down her face. I couldn't even tell if she knew she was crying, Sam. And she kept the act going right up until the time when I left the house. Something is cracking up, Sam. Something is going all to hell, and fast. They seem to be under terrible pressure."

I told her about my espionage activities. I told her I would probably hear from Lou Leeman on Monday. I didn't know if he would report anything that would make any sense.

"How about the Sea Queen?" she asked.

"What about it?"

"It has a number on it so it must be registered somewhere. I wonder if Maurice owns it. And the car."

"Why don't I think of these things? I'll check that out. Build you another drink, Peggy?"

"I don't know. Where are we going?"

"What would you like to do?"

"Well . . . you did mention you have a boat. If it wouldn't be too much trouble to take it out at night . . ."

So I took her out in the Lesser Evil. It's an elderly twenty-foot lapstreak skiff, with an eight-foot beam, stubby foredeck, folding navy top, lots of walkaround. In spite of the heft of the mahogany and white-oak hull, and the matronly beam, the 115 horse Chrysler marine will cruise her at twenty knots, and she'll run dry. She's got an electric bilge pump, self-bailing cockpit and good stowage for gear. The sixty gallon plastic gas tank gives her adequate range. There's a folding captain stool, but there is plenty of freeboard and the steering is set high, so I usually run her standing up, looking over the windshield instead of through it.

After the engine was turning over, I cast off the lines, turned the running lights on, put her in gear and went burbling and mumbling out toward the channel, Peggy standing beside me holding onto the windshield brace.

"It's wonderful!" she said. "Why that name?"

"It's corny and too cute. A couple of years ago I had a thousand bucks saved up. I was feeling restless, and maybe a little depressed. I wanted to fly over to Havana and blow it all on one large binge. But I chose the *Lesser Evil*. I got the hull for four hundred, with a junk engine. I bought the rebuilt Chrysler for three fifty. I put a lot of hours into it. Odds and ends used up the rest of the grand, and a little more."

"Do you use it much?"

"Often enough to be glad I've got it."

"I didn't even know it was such a beautiful night. There's a billion stars, Sam."

"And a moon coming up behind us, girl."

I turned south down the marked channel and I had to use the big spotlight just once to pick up my marker at the turn out through Horseshoe Pass. There was a slight chop in the swash channel, and a gentle swell once we were clear of the pass. I moved out about a half-mile off shore and headed north along the Key. I put the loop of a line on a spoke of the wheel and we went back and sat on the broad transom. We chugged along at dead slow, leaving a phosphorescent wake. The Key beach was a snowy white off the starboard. I pointed out the lights of the Weber place to her, and Ack's place. She found she could look over the side and see the bright streaks made by startled fish.

"Darn it, I wish I'd brought my suit and cap," she said.

"I've got a boarding ladder. You wouldn't have to get

your hair wet. We're in about thirty feet. Easy to anchor."

"Sam, I am often unwise, but not completely damn foolish. I'm not going to put that much strain on our character. The day I go prancing around in my birthday suit will be the day when I'm ready for everything that can happen. Okay?"

"Okay. Next time bring your . . ." A great luminous thrashing and sloshing off the port bow interrupted me. I grabbed a light boat rod from the rack, all rigged and ready with a spoon and trolling weight. I paid the line out over the transom, checked the star drag and gave her the rod. I boosted the throttle and went by the area of violence where the hungry teeth slashed at the school of bait in the moonlight, then swung to port to take the lure through the patch.

I turned and watched her. She stood braced and tense. Suddenly the rod bent and she yelped once and the rod stayed bent and the reel whined as the fish took line against the drag.

"It's a monster! Come help me!"

I laughed at her and told her it was her monster. In a few minutes I knew what it was from the style and frenzy of the runs it made. I kept the engine in neutral, putting it back in gear just a couple of times to swing the stern toward the fish. Each time she would get it close, it would take off again. When it was time, I put on cotton gloves and took a flashlight and went back. I was able to grasp the leader and horse the fish up until I could grab the spoon. I held him up with the light on him.

"What is he? He's beautiful!"

"That's what his name means. Bonito. He'll go about eight or nine pounds. Mackerel family, but inedible. Very black bloody meat."

"Let him go, Sam." I turned the hook upward. He flapped free, splashed into the black water and was gone. "I thought he'd be three times as big as that."

"They're a very strenuous fish."

"How big do they get?"

"I don't know. I think the all tackle record is somewhere around forty pounds."

"He can go tell his wife he had one hell of a strange

experience. Golly, my wrists are practically lame. How long did it take me?"

"Six or seven minutes."

"I would have said it was a whole half-hour."

I took the rod from her, sunk the barb in the cork handle and put it back into the rack.

"I *liked* that, Sam. That was fun! I never thought I'd like to catch a fish. Was I good at it?"

"If there was anything you did do wrong, I can't think of it right now. He was hooked solid, or you'd never gotten a look at him. Some time I'll take you down to the mouth of the Shark River when the baby tarpon are hitting bass plugs. They fight in the water and in the air right over your head."

"You do that . . . some time," she said in a small odd voice.

I had spoken with blissful innocence, without thinking of the implications of what I said. I had spoken out of a subconscious certainty that I would take her to many places, and we would do many things together.

"How about a fast run to a beer joint?" I said heartily. "Let's go!"

I opened it up. I let her take the wheel until we got to the pass. She made some wide open circles, standing the craft on its ear, laughing aloud as she did so. I took her into the bay and headed north along the unofficial channel that hugs the bay side of the Key.

"There's the Weber boat basin," I said, "but I don't see the Sea Queen."

"Oh, it's at a marina, Char told me, getting some work done on it. It should be back soon, she said. She knows how much I enjoyed going out on it with them the last time I was here. But . . . I like this boat better."

"It cost about sixty-nine thousand bucks less, my dear."

We tied up at Tad's Sea-Bar just north of City Bridge, drank some draught beer and were driven out sooner than I expected by too much bad, loud music on the juke, and by the entranced hovering of a young man who, big as a school bus, drunk as an unemployed comedian, had fallen hopelessly in love with Peggy the moment he saw her. It was the sort of thing that had happened so often with

117

Judy that it was a sweet sadness to have it happening again. But I found I had a different attitude about it. In the days of Judy the special attention she received in every public place had tickled my pride in being the chosen escort of such a superb status symbol, and it had also made me feel a deadly and pleasurable willingness to rise and smite any clown who carried admiration one half-step too far.

I was glad to be once again with a girl men admire. (Sis had never wanted to be taken to public places.) But I was pleased for her sake rather than my own. I did not have the feeling of a man bearing a trophy of the chase. And I was not concealing any eagerness to hit anybody. I knew that the change in attitude made me more relaxed and comfortable in public. I wondered if there was the outside chance I might be growing up. In the old days I would have littered the sawdust floor with the burly boy's teeth. Instead I hustled Peggy back aboard the *Lesser Evil* and ran up the main channel toward home under a platinum shimmer of moonlight.

I moored the boat and took the girl home. I blinked my lights twice as I pulled up in front of the Weber house.

"There is one pine tree along the beach I want to see if it is still there," she said rapidly.

"It's the sort of thing we better keep checking on," I agreed.

I was very aware of Luxey off somewhere in the shadows as we walked away from the car. We went up the beach.

"This one, I think it was," Peggy said.

"You're so right," I said, as she lifted her arms and her lips.

I released her after a long warm time of our increasing involvement. "Every night becomes the best night ever," she whispered.

"It's going to be quite a responsibility to keep that up."

"I don't want to be a responsibility. I want to be an old shoe girl. I want to be cozy, dammit. Somebody told me once I have a champagne and stateroom look. I can't help that. I'm more the beer and scow type inside."

"You're a glamorous model. You scare me."

"Do you like the way I look?"

"I like it fine."

"Then it's all right with me too."

I kissed her again and walked her back to the house. I wanted to pick her up earlier Saturday night, but she said she thought the same time would be about right, so she wouldn't feel guilty about leaving Charity alone. I watched her out of sight past the shrubbery at the curve of the front walk, and then got into the car.

Before I could turn the key, Luxey appeared at the side window and said, "Howdy."

"And how are you, Mr. Skull-thumping Depity, sir?"

"That's the prettiest girl I ever seen in my whole life."

"And I suspect she's just as nice as she looks, LeRoy."

"If you mess around with her, Brice, I can make you sorry you ever lived to grow so big."

"Your trouble, LeRoy, is you want to stand guard on the whole world."

"I'll stand guard on my little piece of it, Brice."

"Go catch yourself some prowlers."

"It's grave quiet around here. If Haywood was coming around, he's had plenty of chance afore now. I talked to Mr. Weber and we agreed how this had best be my last night down here."

"I wouldn't want you to be bored, LeRoy."

"Man never gets bored doing his given work, Brice. I was up onto my toes only one time tonight, but it turned out it was just him and her having a fight."

"The Webers? I heard they never fight."

"Then you heard wrong, or they just begun a new habit. I figured somebody maybe snuck by me, but when I found me the right winder I seen it was just the two of them doing all the fussing, in that big bedroom, and her in her stark naked hide, honest to Bess."

"Now you can arrest yourself for being a Peeping Tom, LeRoy."

"I took jest the one look, thinking at first glance she had on little white pants and a little white top thing, but it was where that sun burn leaves off on her. I should

119

think a woman with skin that white would want to stay white and pretty."

"It's a fad, LeRoy."

"I took jest one look like I said and while I was taking in the fact it was a family fuss, I couldn't help seeing she's built awful good for a lady her age I hunkered down under the window and walked away, but not before he shut up all that yelling by smacking her a good one, the way it sounded She cut off in the middle of a word and then she got to moaning some and I heard a door slam."

"What was she yelling about?"

"I don't really know. She was yelling and crying all at once and getting the words all gobbled up the way a female will do, but it was something about not being able to stand any more, or being able to go on. Woman talk. And he give her a man answer." He turned his head and spat. "It's none of your business nor mine, Brice. You can drive on out of here any time."

So I said good night to the savage little man and drove away, leaving him to his sleepless, restless, silent prowling.

Chapter Eight

On SATURDAY morning I had an early call from an adjustor in Tampa, and I had to make one appraisal in Venice and one in Punta Gorda, which used up all of the morning, because I had to track the Punta Gorda car through three different stops before I caught up with it.

I went back to the office after lunch, wrote out my reports in longhand for Alice to type up, made up a mail deposit of accumulated checks for appraisal fees, balanced my check book and brought my expense records up to date. Cal McAllen phoned me just as I was leaving, so I drove over to town and went up to his office.

I hadn't seen him since Tuesday. The four days had marked him. There was a gray look to his skin. The bone structure of his face looked more prominent. His eyes seemed to have sunk back into his head.

He was apologetic. "I hope I haven't inconvenienced you, Sam. I haven't got any new information. It's driving me out of my mind. I just wanted to talk to somebody about her. I can't talk to her family. They act like I'm an interloper."

"When there's trouble, that Gantry family gets very tight knit."

"I've arranged with Pat Millhaus to put up five thousand dollars for information regarding her whereabouts. It will be in this evening's paper."

"That should bring in a lot of crackpot assistance."

"They're getting a lot of wild tips already, Sam. They're checking them all out. One man claims he saw them, Sis and that Haywood, going aboard a freighter over in Ever-

121

glades City. They ran a radio check on that one, and it was a forty year old Brazilian woman and her son on their way home to Rio. Damn it, Sam, I just . . ."

"Waiting is the hardest thing we're ever asked to do, Cal."

"Have you had any other ideas at all?"

I suppose I could have briefed him on what I was doing, with Peggy's help. But there wasn't anything specific as yet. And I suspected that in his anxiety he was not capable of handling any delicate situation. He would charge in, yelling and waving his arms, glad of the release.

We talked for a little while longer. After I left his office I was aware of something buried so deeply in my mind I could not get at it. Something I had been told did not fit with the other information. The oyster solves her problem of granular irritation by coating the offending object with pearl juice. But the unidentifiable little object in my mind kept sliding around, scratchy and obstinate. When I tried to get a good look at it, it moved out of reach.

I took my problem to a drugstore counter and, after a second cup of stale-tasting coffee I began to get the feeling that it was a problem of timing. I wrote out a little schedule on the back of an envelope:

August 10—Charlie escapes (Wednesday)
　　　 12—Two men arrive at Webers (Friday night)
　　　 14—Charlie arrives at my place (Sunday)
　　　 15—Charlie and Sis disappear (Mon. night)
　　　 16—Two men leave (Tues. night)
　　　 17—Peggy arrives (Wed. late afternoon)

I stared blankly at my timetable. There was one inference that could be made. The newspapers had covered Charlie Haywood's escape. Maurice Weber could have yelled for help as soon as he learned of the escape. The two men could have arrived in answer to the yell, ready to take care of Charlie if and when he showed up. And if he did show up Monday night and if they did take care of him, then they could leave on Tuesday night, mission accomplished.

But it wasn't what was bothering me. Suddenly I realized what it was. I added one more item to my list.

August 16—Millhaus checks Weber house (Tues. morning)

I went right to the Florence County House. It was a little after three in the afternoon, and the air had become very still and heavy. Thunderheads were piled massive and high over the Gulf, grumbling toward the mainland.

I had to wait twenty minutes before I could see him. By the time I got into his office, the sunshine outside his window had a coppery look and the separate thumps of thunder were spaced and identifiable.

Pat waved me to a chair, a smile of habitual contempt on his Indian-looking face. He wore a green sports shirt unbuttoned to the waist, exposing a chest thatched hard and black, with one irregular patch of white centered between the brute nipples, a patch as big as a grapefruit. His face and chest glistened as though he had been sprayed with glycerine.

"Hot one," he said. "Damn if I can even get a room air conditioner approved. Man can't think so good with his brains steaming. Luxey tells me you got the hots for a pretty little house guest out to the Weber place. You keep her out all night, he says. A big hero like you, when one shack job turns up missing, you don't waste no time lining up something else."

I stared at him. "What makes you so damn miserable, Pat?"

"It's a funny thing, Sam. Everybody on the wrong side of the law comes up with the idea I'm miserable. But I play poker regular with some of the biggest men in this county and they like me just fine."

"What gives you the idea I'm on the wrong side of the law?"

"A man works around the law long enough, he gets the knack of picking out the bad ones. You've got no record yet, Sam. Maybe you've been too cute to get caught. Maybe you haven't had the nerve to do anything worse than try to throw a ball game. But I got the comfortable feel-

123

ing you and I, we stay in the same county long enough, one day I'm going to be able to ride on out and watch you swinging a brush hook on the County Road Gang."

"For God's sake, Millhaus, I'm more honest than you are!"

He leaned his beefy arms on the desk. "Just get it through your head, Sam, we're talking across a fence, me on one side, you on the other. Now what the hell do you want?"

"I came to ask you a question. Last Tuesday morning you checked the Weber house and grounds."

"What's that to you?"

"Who all was there, at the house, Pat?"

He leaned back and looked at me with distaste. "I got the funny idea you're trying to mess into this thing, Brice."

"I'm just asking a question."

"I'd surely love to find out you're doing some investigating without having a license for it."

"Sis is my friend. It's normal curiosity. Cal McAllen has normal curiosity too. So does her family."

"The Webers give me complete cooperation, Brice. They cooperated fine when Haywood got sent up. They cooperated fine the other day. I'm satisfied they don't figure in this thing at all."

"Then why not tell me who was at the house?"

The last of the sun went suddenly and the world darkened and, after the few first, fat, random drops, the rain came down in a great roaring wash, with blue crack of lightning and busy artillery barrage of thunder. Pat jumped up and adjusted his windows and turned on the desk light. It dimmed and went out.

He raised his voice above the storm. "At the house was the Webers and that Kraut couple and the boat captain."

"And house guests?"

"I was told so, but I didn't see 'em. There was a rental car there. The house guests were on the beach, I was told."

"You had no chance to question them, then?"

"Why the hell should I? Mr. and Mrs. Weber, they

124

said everybody had gone to bed early on Monday night and nobody had heard a thing. Goddammit, Brice, get your nose the hell out of my job or I sure as hell will book you for obstructing justice."

"Isn't there a lot of pressure on you about this thing?"

"Are you worried about me?"

"You should welcome any constructive interest in it, Pat."

"Why don't you run for sheriff, you silly bastard? Don't tell me how to do my job."

"So where do you think Sis Gantry is?"

"I can tell you just where she is, Brice. Haywood knew the Gantry family well. He knew Sis would come on the run to help anybody she felt needed her. You should know. That's the same approach you used, isn't it?"

"If you know everything there is to know, you don't have to ask."

"So he phoned her and she went out in that little car and picked him up someplace, and on account of he was a mess from five days in the swamps, her heart went out to him. He had to have some place to hide, right? So she taken him back into the back country someplace. That girl used to hunt with her brothers. She takes him back to some shack and once they got there, he took charge and he won't let her loose, afraid she'll be questioned and give something away. And he hasn't had his hands on a woman in over two years, so that's something you got to figure too. He's got the little car covered up with brush, and when all the fuss dies down, he's going to take off north and try to get out of the state, and maybe he'll let her loose and maybe he'll kill her."

"What are they doing for food and water, Pat?"

"When she left the house she had maybe fifty dollars in her purse. She left the house a little after eight. There's little grocery stores all over the area that're hungry enough to stay open late. It's none of your damn business but we've been checking them out, Sam, and some woman bought about forty dollars worth of stuff around nine o'clock closing time at a little store north of town. The owner that waited on her doesn't have the faintest idea of what she looked like on account of he's had one cata-

125

ract operation and he's due for the next and he can't get used to the glasses, so he kind of operates his little store by touch and memory. He doesn't remember much of the order, except there was a lot of staples in it, sugar, salt, flour and so on. I figure she thought she was picking up that stuff for Haywood, not knowing he wasn't going to let her loose once she took him to a good place to hide out and get rested up."

"If he wanted to run, Pat, why did he come back here?"

"You'd make a poor sheriff if you can't figure that out. It was the direction where he figured we'd do the least looking. And where else could he go to find anybody to give him some help?"

It had a considerable amount of weight. Suppose when Sis had phoned Charity Weber at Charlie's request, while I was spying on them through the window, Charity had refused to talk to Charlie, or, if Sis had been trying to trick Charity into a situation where she couldn't help seeing Charlie, she had suspected what was happening. Then it might have happened just as Pat assumed.

"Now get out," he said, "and don't come back wasting my time."

I went out and waited in the doorway until the rain let up, and then ran to my car. I had cleverly left the windows open and the front seat was awash. I wiped it reasonably dry with a rag. The last of the rain moved east and the sun was out again. Steam drifted up from all the streets. There was an illusion of freshness in the air, and the scent of wet lush soil, hot damp pavement.

Three blocks from the courthouse I discarded Pat Millhaus's theory. It was not within the range and limits of Sis's character not to let her people know she was all right. And it was not conceivable that Charlie Haywood could have wanted to or been able to restrain her forcibly. All persons are imprisoned by their own moral and ethical standards. Never, except in madness, do they step beyond their own limitations.

At quarter after four I decided to go take a look at the *Sea Queen*. It was an idle impulse. I'd never seen her close up. And I realized it might be an easier way to check ownership.

126

I had a choice of several marinas, but I remembered that it had been repaired previously at Jimson's. I turned off the main road a mile north of my place and drove over to the bay front. Though it has gradually turned into a big operation, Jimson's retains a look of clutter, rust, decay and indifference. The sheds and bigger buildings are clustered in a haphazard way. Their big docks need new pilings. They have covered storage, both fresh and salt water. They have a good deep channel and they can haul anything up to seventy feet, run it inside on cradle and tracks and rebuild it, if you have money enough. They have the best marine engine mechanics in the area, good franchises, and a pricing policy that has made strong men weep.

On that Saturday afternoon there was the usual aimless, dogged activity you find around any big boat yard, a whining of saws and sanders, clang of engine tools being dropped on concrete, sharp odors of varnish, paint, gasoline and solvent. Owners were working on their own boats, and the yard employees were working on contract tasks.

I wandered around without anybody paying the slightest attention to me until I found the *Sea Queen*. She was at that covered dock space where repairs are made, sitting in a slip with her stern to the dock. A man in dirty khaki shorts and a blue baseball cap was fitting a new section of railing at the starboard corner of the transom. He slipped the freshly shaped piece of mahogany into place. He was a small old man with a knotted brown back.

He turned and looked at me and grinned, exposing a crying need for expensive dentistry and said, "Well now! Ha-you, Sammy?"

"Hello, J. B. I thought you were in a rocking chair, living off your grandchildren."

"That's surely where I'd like to be. But old Jimson, he sweet talks me into working myself right to the edge of the grave, saying he can't get people to do good work any more. And he can't, by God. But it gives him fits how I won't work on no production line boats. It shames me to touch one of them shoddy things. I'll only work

127

on boats that're put together honest in the first place."

"This is the Weber boat, isn't it, J. B.?"

"Yep." He took the piece of railing over to his work bench, sanded one end carefully, brought it back and tapped it carefully into place with a padded mallet. "Ought to do it," he said.

"It's a perfect match, J. B."

"Has to be, if I do it." He examined the bit in an electric drill, and began to drill for the screws that would hold the section in place.

"What happened to it, J. B.?"

"It was being brung into a dock at low tide, with the wind and current tricky, and the stern swung under the dock and the rail got splintered and bent all to hell, Sammy. Shame to have happen to a boat gets the care this one does."

"Care if I go aboard and look at her?"

"Don't matter to me none, but if that Chase fella comes back when you're aboard, he could turn up ugly. He left when the rain started and didn't say if he was coming back. He don't say much of anything. Your daddy, he was a quiet man, but not the same way. Your daddy liked other folks to be talking, but Chase don't want much to do with the human race, it looks like. It's a relief to have him gone for a while. He watches every damn move I make."

I went aboard. It was fifty-four feet of luxury and had every navigation aid known except radar. It was equipped with air conditioning and television and a handsome flying bridge. It took me about two minutes to find the log and the papers. There are very few logical places to keep such items aboard any boat. The listed owner was Starr Development. I checked below fast and furtive as a thief. When I stepped back onto the dock, I knew what was wrong with the Sea Queen. The Webers had been using her for over four years. But they'd left no mark on her. There were some clothes, toilet articles, liquor and food stowed neatly aboard, and there was an oversize bunk in the master stateroom neatly made up, but it looked as though they had used it for four weeks rather than four years. And only obsessive maintenance could have kept the below decks and topsides in such perfect and shining condition.

J. B. was countersinking brass screws into the new section of rail. "Good shape, isn't she?"

"The best."

"Funny things, Sammy. This much boat is for cruising. Marathon, Nassau, all over hell and gone. They use it often, but they don't go noplace. Hell, the way they use it, they could get along with that little punkin seed you got."

"Leave my boat out of this, old man."

A battered yellow motor scooter chugged along the dock area toward us. "You got off her just in time, Sammy," J. B. muttered.

The man parked the scooter on its brace and walked over without glancing at either of us. He walked directly to the section of rail, ran the palm of his hand across the two joinings, bent to inspect it inch by inch.

He made a grunting sound which I thought was supposed to express approval. "Sure it's seasoned good?" he asked J. B.

"It's top grade."

"I'll do the finishing on it myself."

"When you come to rubbing it down between coats, you'd best use . . ."

"I know how." It wasn't said with irritation or anger. It was said to inform J. B. that no help was needed. "Set those last couple screws and I'll take her along now."

"It's a nice craft," I said amiably.

He turned and gave me one quick glance of appraisal and dismissal. He was a solidly-built man in his forties with a face like carved dark stone, with weather wrinkles that turned his eyes to bright blue slits. He had a look of competence, self-sufficiency. He turned away without an answer and I knew he would never answer the casual comment. He did not need conversation with strangers. If I were going to pry him open, it would have to be with some other method.

"Too damn nice," I said with manufactured indignation, "for some clown to bash her into a dock. That's what keeps the yards going, the people that don't know

129

how to handle a boat." I would have thought he wasn't hearing a word if I hadn't seen the back of his neck slowly deepening in color.

"When they got enough money they don't have to bash their boats up themselves," I said. "They can hire some guy to do it for them."

That brought him around to face me, his eyes more slitted than before, his jaw muscles working, brown fists clenched. "And just what kind of a license do you hold, mister?"

"I don't hold any. But I've been handling boats since I was four years old and I never shoved one half under a dock yet, friend."

"Shove off, mister."

"J. B., this comedy captain is talking rough to me. Friend of yours?"

"Let's not have any fussing going on," J. B. said.

"If a man racks up a boat he ought to be man enough to admit it."

Captain Stan Chase took a slow step toward me. "I didn't damage the boat."

"What got to it? Big termites maybe?"

"I wasn't aboard."

It startled me. "I thought you ran this Matthews for the Webers."

"I do. And when I do, mister, nothing happens to it. Nothing!"

"Then it looks like you should run it all the time, friend."

"I always have. Except this one time."

I could sense that the injury to the boat was as painful to him as a wound in his own flesh. This was basically a shy man, a quiet man, perhaps a good man.

"It's too much boat for an amateur," I said.

"He's run it a lot when I've been aboard. He knows how to handle it pretty good. But not at night. It's too tricky at night. He shouldn't have tried it."

"Good as new," J. B. said, "once you put the finish on it." He patted the rail. "You're all set now, Captain."

"If you didn't think he could handle it," I said, "why didn't you go along?"

For several long seconds I thought he wasn't going to answer. "I wasn't even there," he said. He spat down into the shadowy green water of the bay. "They sent me up to Tampa to meet her sister coming in on a night flight. But she wasn't on that flight. She didn't get in until Wednesday. They had their wires crossed."

"Last Monday night?" I asked.

"Yes. So what?"

I shrugged. There was more that I wanted to ask. But I couldn't go any further without making him suspicious. Why was he sent instead of Mahler? At what time did they ask him to leave?

He spread a length of tarp and wheeled his motor scooter aboard and laid it down gently on the tarp. J.B. and I helped with the lines. He eased the *Sea Queen* expertly out of the slip, rounded the Jimson marker and took her out to the main channel and turned south toward her home berth.

"Bet he hasn't talked that much in a full year," J. B. said, stowing his tools. "You stung him some, Sammy."

"I tried to."

"What good did it do?"

"I've just got a mean nature, J. B."

"Well, if you have, you surely got the looks to go with it."

I went home and showered and stretched out on my bed. The rain had brought the toads out and they were in good voice. Bugs, mourning doves and mocking birds were trying to drown them out. I felt tired but not sleepy. When the phone rang, it was D. Ackley Bush.

"Dear boy, thank you so much for returning the shell, but what made you think you could avoid giving me a progress report?"

"Wouldn't you rather wait for a complete story?"

"Nonsense! You have been seen in the company of a young and lovely stranger. Who is she?"

"Sort of a sister of Mrs. Weber's, Ack. The same one who spent two weeks visiting her last summer."

"And I didn't know?"

"Apparently not."

"I often wonder if one can become senile without being terrible aware of it, Samuel."

"Your very best friends wouldn't tell you."

"Why are you so elusive, my boy? Is the sister succumbing to those charms I have never been able to perceive?"

"We have become buddies."

"Which is, of course, a much more effective way of learning all the secrets of the Weber household. Perhaps you have the conspiratorial knack, Samuel."

"Me? I'm just dating a fine item."

"Come and tell me all you've learned, dear boy."

"I haven't learned a thing that would interest you."

"I can be very interested by very minor things. And how would you know what fragments of information are significant? You need to enlist a better mind than yours to sort out all the bits and pieces."

"Later on, Ack. Maybe. But not yet."

"You are very stubborn."

"I'll be in touch, later on."

I heard him sigh. "I know. Don't phone me; I'll phone you."

By three minutes after nine I was parked in a very dark place with my arms around Peggy Varden, and for that little space of time the world made very good sense. She wanted the same kind of evening as before, which showed superb judgment.

She made her report as we were heading for the cottage. "Absolutely nothing today, Sam. A perfect empty blah. Char has been out of circulation most of the day. She fell last night, somehow, and hurt her face. Her left eye is puffed almost shut and she feels miserable."

"Maurice put the slug on her."

"I'd like to think so, but they don't ever get that . . . emotional."

I told her about LeRoy's report of the incident. She was astonished.

"It must be true! Golly, Sam, they must be cracking up."

I gave her all the rest of it after we were on my porch with the lights adjusted, music playing, tall drinks in

132

hand. I told her all I could remember about the conversations I'd had with Cal McAllen, Pat Millhaus, Captain Stan Chase.

"When I heard the boat coming I went out. I helped a little with the lines, but he was so sour about it I gave up. He likes to do everything himself. He rigged a canvas thing over the railing and he was working out there until dark, refinishing the new part."

"Now I've got some specific things I want you to find out, Peggy. I don't know if you can. But don't press if you run into a block. Okay?"

"Okay. No pressing."

"I'd like to know just when Chase was told to go to Tampa. I think Sis made that phone call at about eight-thirty, maybe a few minutes later. If they had an airline timetable in the house . . ."

"I know they do. I've seen one."

"Good. Then, if they wanted Chase out of the way, they could look up a likely flight and send Chase up there in the Lincoln to meet it. And he would have gotten his orders after Sis talked to Charity. Now I wonder if the Mahlers would be sent anywhere too."

"But they wouldn't have to be."

"Why not?"

"They're usually through by eight-thirty, Sam, and they hole up in their own apartment beyond the garage. Herman is getting a little bit deaf. They keep the television on loud, and I do mean loud. Their draperies are always pulled shut and, besides, their windows face north. Once they're on their own time, they never come back into the main part of the house, or even set foot outside."

"And that would leave Sis and Charlie alone with the Webers and the two house guests."

"I don't like this kind of . . . hinting," she said in a very small voice.

"Not hinting. Thinking out loud. But the direction I'm going makes me feel sick."

She came over to my chair. "Make a lap. The way you sound, Sam, I want arms around me, if you're going to keep on talking."

133

I took her onto my lap and held her snug. "You've guessed what I have to say, Peggy. Two people and a small car are missing. That's a big boat. It was taken out on that same Monday night. A section of rail was smashed."

She rocked her round forehead against the angle of my jaw. "I don't like it, Sam."

"One big section of rail is detachable, wide enough to roll the car aboard. But out in the Gulf, with some roll and pitch, it wouldn't be as easy to deep-six it."

She straightened up. "But why not just run the little car into the water!"

"Where? These are shallow waters. No cliffs, no natural holes close to shore."

She shivered and tilted her mouth up and I gave her a kiss of comfort. But it turned into a lot more than was intended until finally she wrenched away and jumped up. "That makes me feel ashamed, Sam. We're talking about a horrible murder, and all of a sudden we're . . . necking. And I feel so . . . responsive. What kind of monsters are we? Are we that callous?"

"We're that human, Peggy. Fire, flood, war, disaster. One emotion seems to take the lid off the others. It's a sort of affirmation. We have to prove we're alive. Maybe it isn't in the best taste in the world, but it isn't shameful. Come on back."

"No thanks. Not right now. Don't be annoyed with me, Sam."

"How could I be? Look, maybe I'm getting too intricate and gaudy about all this. It's been building, bit by bit, in the back of my mind and now I can't think of anything else, so maybe it's time to check it all out."

"But how?"

"Go to Jimson's and look over the scrap J. B. discarded. And you could do something if you've got the stomach for it. This is the rainy season. The ground is soft. They couldn't carry the Renault to the dock. They could have rolled the tire marks out, but not all of them. Look for tire marks, probably, because of the Mahlers, on the south side of the house."

She came back to my lap with a great sigh. "I can't

134

believe it, really." She nestled against my throat. "I don't want to believe a horrible thing like that about Charity!"

"There were some handy helpers, remember. And you said she's so nervous and restless you think she's cracking up. I don't want to believe it either. But when two people and a car drop off the edge of the world, you can assume a damn efficient disposal system."

"Who would believe us?"

"Nobody, yet. We have to find something specific to back it up, or we may come across something that proves we're wrong."

"Isn't it time for us to get some . . . professional help?"

"Like from my old Sheriff-buddy-pal?"

"Well . . . I guess that wouldn't be so hot."

"There is one thing I can and will do right now, Peggy. And don't you try to put up any battle, girl."

"Sir!"

"That isn't what I've got on my mind . . . yet. Whether this boat guess is right or wrong, Peggy, you are living in a creepy and deteriorating situation. It's no place for you to be. So just do this final bit of checking tomorrow, and get yourself inconspicuously packed, and I'll come around in the late afternoon and take you away from there."

"But what will I tell Charity!"

"I don't care what you tell her."

"She's my sister."

"Theres no blood relationship at all."

"I'm perfectly safe there, Sam, really I am."

"I'm taking no chances with you. None."

"Mmmm. It's that important, huh?"

"Yes.'

"Then I guess you'd better locate me a nice cheap, clean, little motel deal, my darling. Because I've got a lot of vacation left. And it is my humble desire to cater to your most foolish little whim. If you don't want me there, I leave."

"Suddenly I feel one hell of a lot better."

"And you make me feel sort of valuable. And sort of protected."

"I wish you didn't have to go back at all."

"Oh, I have to look for tire tracks."

"Of course. Tire tracks."

"Dearest, you have the most gigantic hands. The most gigantic and sneaky hands. So let's ride in your boat and cool you off. Let's go very fast in your boat."

There was a special gaiety for a time, as though we were both running from a blackness in the backs of our minds. On that night she wore yellow-green slacks and a Guatemalan blouse of coarse cotton, and she laughed often. We went again to Tad's Sea-Bar. The jukebox volume was down, the draught beer chill, and her enormous admirer was absent. With very little warning all the sparkle and vitality went out of her. I had seen it happen so many times with Judy that I made the wrong assumption that it would be just the same with Peggy, that she had gone beyond my reach, back into some moody cave, and any attempt to reach her would only increase the remoteness.

But this Peggy looked directly into my eyes and placed her hand on mine and said, "I'm sorry, darling. I'm down a deep well. Help me climb out."

"How?"

"Lets go, right now."

I drove the *Lesser Evil* back down the bay through moonlight, and she stood in the half circle of my right arm, leaning against me, slightly huddled and very subdued. "It got to me," she said. "It didn't seem fair to be laughing and to be in . . ."

"Be in what?"

"Darn it! Darn it! Am I not a woman of total mystery, darn it?"

"Be in what?"

"Stop teasing me like that. I was not fishing. And I didn't know what I was going to say until I almost said it, and you know very well what I almost said. I'm blushing and you're making it worse. It's up to the man to be the first one to say a darn thing like that."

"You couldn't possibly have been going to say be in love!"

"Sam Brice. I'm going to belt you one, right in the chops."

"This love routine, they give it a pretty big play. The songs and so forth."

She backed away to get a little room, and kicked me squarely in the shin. I throttled down immediately, knocked the lever into neutral, gathered her in and kissed her with a glad and total emphasis. I put my hands on her narrow waist and lifted her up and sat her on the small shelf effect above the instrument panel, her back to the slant of the windshield. I held her hands and looked up at her face in moonlight. Her small chin was level with my eyes.

"Okay, Peggy," I said. "Love. I'm sure. I'm very sure."

"I'm sure too. And I'm scared."

"Of what?"

"It was love before. Can you accept that and not be jealous?"

"Of course."

"And it was such a horrible, hurtful, shattering loss, I didn't ever want to be . . . committed in the same way again, darling. I didn't want any man to be at the center of my life. I . . . thought I wanted another marriage, but to a man who would love me and not ask for too much involvement on my part. So he could be at the edge of my life, so nothing could ever hurt me so badly again."

"But you couldn't find him."

"I looked."

"But you're one of the unfortunates, Peggy? All or nothing."

"Yes. I can't seem to . . . maneuver my life."

"I wasn't looking for this either."

"I know."

"I made the total offering. But the princess decided the dish wasn't so special after all, so she quit nibbling and walked away. So I said the hell with it. If they don't want me—invaluable, unique me—I'll pull the welcome mat in and close the door. And if you train yourself not to think of any of the things that hurt your pride, you can be pretty comfortable counting off the years, honey."

"And a horrid waste of Sam Brice."

"So I re-enter the lists, eh? I go looking for dragons again."

She kissed my lips quickly, lightly. "Sam, Sam, not for me. All I want is love. Kindly leave off the tail fins and the country club. Do no more and no less than you want to do, Sam. Keep a roof over me. Keep me warm. Keep me fed. Keep me barefoot and pregnant. Rat races are for rats, not people. I'm terribly glad and I'm still scared."

"I don't deserve this much luck. I am going to risk making you sore, Peggy. But right now I know something and I have to say it."

"You know you can say anything in the world to me."

"There have been two women in my life who have meant anything to me. Judy and Sis. In some crazy way you're the best of both of them. I needed them only because I didn't know I was looking for you."

She grabbed at me in an almost spasmodic way and pulled my head against her breast, against a precious roundness and warmth and a scented sweetness under the coarse cotton. "Sore at you?" she whispered. "If I'd missed hearing that I'd have never forgiven you. Mmmm. This is what it's like, isn't it?"

"This is the product they keep plugging."

"Darling?"

"Yes?"

"Mmmm. What is that sort of expensive kind of grinding noise?"

"Oh. We've drifted out of the channel. We're just rubbing on an oyster bar."

"Is that good?"

"Most people don't like it at all."

"I'll fix it. I come with dowry, you know. Three grand, practically. All saved, but I didn't know for what. I didn't know it would be for boat repairs."

"How quick can you get up there and get back with the money?"

"Crass greedy pig!"

I untangled myself and lifted her down and checked the depth off the stern with the boat hook. I sent her to the stern to change the weight distribution and backed off with care and moved back into the channel.

I moored the boat at my dock and we walked hand in hand to the cottage. "I could go up with you," I said.

"I don't want to go anywhere in the world that's more

than fifty feet from you, Sam. But I better go up first and kind of wind up the chapter entitled Richmond."

"How long would that take?"

"Two to three weeks, because I do want to be considerate. Peter's uncle has been so wonderful."

"I guess you'd want to be married in Dayton?"

We were at the porch door. "I'd like that very much, Sam."

"This is the slack season in my business, so when you leave here, why don't we go direct to Dayton. I'll meet your folks and do what has to be done about licenses in Ohio. Then you go to Richmond and I'll come back here. Then when you're ready to whistle, I'll buzz back to Dayton."

"Right!" she said briskly. She stook her hand out. "Seeing as how we're engaged, mister, let's shake hands."

We shook hands solemnly. "That hair is meant for moonlight," I said.

"Let's not stand out here, son. I feel like Apple Mary. Take me in."

We went in and I dug into the back of a cupboard and found a bottle of Chablis. It seemed to be a time for wine. And no time to cool it, so we had it on the rocks. Peggy called it a very low way to drink wine.

We pulled the two porch chairs close together and held hands and drank wine and looked at the moonlight.

"It was the raccoon," she said dreamily. "That white lady raccoon. That's when I started to fall in love."

"I'm a more basic type. I began to get the general idea while kneading a fine leg."

"It hurt so much I didn't have any room to think about how . . . darn undignified it was."

"Just don't be scared," I told her. "That's all. We've been off to stormy, thorny places, and now we're back, and this is where life is."

We sat in the silence of one A.M., and it was not a silence at all, not with the slap of mullet in the bay, a hot shrill frenzy of the night bugs, a compulsive self-adulation of mocking birds.

My girl sighed and said, "I'm a lousy bad manager."

"Indeed?"

"I have been toying with the idea of something cute.

139

Like maybe going inside and then calling you to come find me in your bed, and me saying peekaboo or something equally girlish. Like an affirmation. Like saying to you, see how I trust you and I'm not scared. But things shouldn't be shoved along too fast. Lordy, they go fast enough as is!"

"Peggy, you are a strain on my nerves."

"Then, you see, I'd need to have you tell me that the whole routine wasn't the least bit coarse, hasty, or sordid, that I was enchanting, and love justifies everything, and we've both been married, and so on. You know?"

"Go get ready and I'll practice my lines."

"I am not going to be elfin and nervous, which I couldn't help being here and now."

"And I'd probably bumble and stammer."

"But—Sam, find a dandy motel, Sam."

"Summer rates."

"When I go north to change lives, I don't want to be wondering about us in any way at all. Call it a seal of approval or something. And forgive me right now for being a conniving bitch instead of a spontaneous one. Okay?"

I set my glass down, caught her by the wrist and brought her over into my lap, kissed her until, when I released her, her breathing was long, deep, humid, audible. "Sam," she whispered, "you're making the pants too long."

There is only one way to handle a remark like that. I stood her up, laid the heft of my hand smartly on the seat of the pretty slacks and took her, giggling, to the car and back to the Weber house.

Chapter Nine

I SLEEP LATE on Sunday, and woke to a blazing day. I made myself an ornate breakfast, and I kept catching myself humming, whistling and smiling in a broad and fatuous way. It was noon before I got around to prying J. B. loose from his bachelor shack in the piney woods and taking him to Jimson's. He didn't know what I had in mind, but he was willing to go along with it, after expressing what he felt was sufficient irritation.

Once we were there it took about twenty minutes to locate the scrapped fragments of the rail off the *Sea Queen.*

"How did the damage look when you saw it, J. B.?"

"I looked it over, Sammy, and I figured there was only one way it could have happened. The stern swung under a dock, and there was a swell, and as whoever was running it tried to swing the stern back out, fast, the swell brought it up against the underside of the dock."

"So that the rail was broken away from the boat?"

"Hell, you can see that from this junk here, Sammy. This here tube bronze was the upright supports, and they was bent outwards all to hell, this-a-way."

I went over the bent metal inch by inch in the bright sunlight. I found the abrasion, with black enamel ground into it.

"I want to take this piece along, J. B."

"I don't guess old Jimson will ever miss the scrap value onto it. Why the hell do you want it, Sammy?"

"If it ever comes up, J. B., will you testify that this piece came off the *Sea Queen?*"

141

"It better not come up on account of I don't like court stuff. Is this some part of your insurance job, Sammy?"

"Sort of."

I put the twisted section of tubing in the wagon. I no longer had any doubt but what a spectroscopic analysis would prove the black shear was paint off a Renault. I tried to keep my attitude objective. I knew that if my imagination started working, I was going to feel very, very sick.

I took J. B. back to his place, and then drove down to Maria's Bar in Bayside. It is a shabby joint patronized almost exclusively by commercial fishermen. There is no group more clannish, more violent or more callously exploited. As it was well after one o'clock, the place was beginning to fill up with the Sunday afternoon trade. I had known some of these men all my life. And even though, as a kid, I had endured the backbreak of the gill nets, working on shares, I was still an outsider, and I knew I had to move slowly and carefully. I could not hope to start a conversation.

After I had made two beers last the best part of an hour, a man named Jaimie France moved over to stand beside me. I had known him in high school. We made small talk, and I slipped with no conscious effort into the slow, easy diction of long ago.

"You know that Sea Queen?" I asked him. "Big Matthews from the south end of Horseshoe."

"I know that one. Bettern fifty foot. Fella name of Chase operates it."

"Jaimie, do you think I could find anybody that'd know if she went out the pass there last Monday night?"

He waited for me to give a reason for wanting to know, and when I gave no reason, he asked for none. That, too, is part of the code of behavior.

"Any special time Monday night?" he asked.

"Around ten, maybe, but it could've been sooner or later."

"Would depend if anybody was off the pass that night, Sam. Let me check around some."

He sauntered away and it was ten minutes before he came back to the end of the bar with a tall gnarled old man whose weathered face was familiar to me, but whose name I could not remember.

"You know Sam Brice, Luke," Jaimie said.

"Knew his daddy," the old man said.

"This here is Luke Johnson," Jaimie said. I shook a hand that was like stones wrapped in leather. "Says he saw her Monday night."

"Can I buy you a drink, Mr. Johnson?"

"Don't mind if I do." After it was ordered, the old man said, "Me and the boys was a quarter-mile off the pass, just south a ways, pootling along slow outside that big bar, looking for to net moonlight mackerel if we could find a school surfacing good when my youngest, he said, "Now what the hell do you figure he's doing over there, Pa?' We all looked and it was a big one coming out the pass without a speck of light showing on her noplace, going along damn near wide open. Now you know the way that pass is silting, you got one way to go out straight or you can feel your way along the swash, but if you draw up to three feet and more, you can mess yourself up good, and it looked like he was going right for that bar on the north. We stood a-looking at him and we kinda sucked in, the way you do when you figure somebody's going to hit, but it was coming on high tide and he had damn fool luck and got over where there couldn'ta been more'n one inch of water under the hull.

"Me and the boys we talked over who it coulda been and it looked like that Sea Queen Matthews you been asking Jaimie about, but we decided it was maybe some stranger on account of Chase knows that pass real good, and my middle boy said the above decks looked wrong somehow when he caught her in silhouette in the moonlight, and my middle boy has a good eye."

"Did he say what looked wrong about it, Mr. Johnson?"

"Said it looked like it had a little fantail cabin stuck onto it."

"What did it do?"

"Went right on straight out, clean outa sight. We worked our way north and come onto mackerel maybe a mile north of the pass. We were busy on the nets and it was maybe forty minutes later my oldest pointed out

143

something coming back into the pass with the running lights on, big enough to be that Matthews again, but going a lot slower than coming out."

He could add nothing else. I thanked him, and he thanked me, with decorum and dignity, for his drink, and went back to his friends.

"One time way back," Jaimie said, "some folks at Boca that had a hired captain got drunk and took a big Chris out at night, and damn if they didn't run it right up into the mangrove on LaCosta Key, wide open, half killing a couple that was up on the bow making love at the time."

I didn't rise to that bait, and I left as soon as I could do so without offending Jaimie France.

As I drove back toward town I knew I had enough to take to the law. It all fitted together too neatly. No matter what Pat Millhaus thought of me personally, he would have to move on the basis of the evidence I would give him. But first I had to go get my girl.

I would get her and take her to Captain's Cove and rent one of those properly secluded cabanas for my girl. I felt the sweet twist of desire for her, and it was good. But this was for more than that alone, for more than the old pulse and tangle of flesh, the usage of bodies. There would be that, yes. I knew we both sensed how fine that would be, and both wanted it and soon. But it would be icing on our cake. This was a walking girl, for hot beaches and rainy streets; a talking girl, for private times and quiet places; a loving girl to do things for, who would return all small favors and affections in a hundred ways; a warm and healthy girl, eager to become heavy with child.

I parked in the mouth of the Weber driveway and touched the horn ring, then got out and walked to the front door. I pressed the bell button and looked at my watch. Twenty after five. I had heard no sound inside the house. I pressed it again.

Charity Weber opened the door halfway. "Well now!" she said in her whispery growl of a voice. "Howdy," she said. She made a few small muscular adjustments to her figure, and gave me all the show biz projection, with a garrulity of eyebrows.

144

"Hi. I want to see Peggy."

"Come on in and I'll call her," she said. She was not very convincing. She seemed to be under great stress, so that her attempts to be super-charming seemed like an automatic afterthought.

She stepped back and I went in. I sensed somebody at my left. I started to turn my head. Something made a very small sound. Whish. My head was blown off. Fragments of it soared back through my childhood, arching and fizzing. The rest of me went down a long greased slide, naked and belly-down, down into blackness . . .

. . . . a kitten trapped under the house, mewling, homesick, lost. A faint sad sound reaching down into my sleep. I wanted it to go away. I would not come up out of my good sleep. And in its whinings, the kitten formed my name. "Oh, Sam!" it said. "Oh, darling." In the illogic of dreams I could accept that . . . almost. Certainly kittens can talk, I told myself. Do not be excited about it. But logic festered in small ways, and I began to come up out of the black comfort, up to a sick sweat, pain, a gray world.

I was on my back, my head turned toward the right. I opened my eyes and saw a cinderblock wall inches away, in that faint gray light that can be dawn or dusk. The whole left side of my head felt ballooned by pain, so that I could imagine my ear was a dozen inches beyond where it should have been. I wanted to touch the area with great care, great concern. But my hands were numb and clumsy clubs, bound together. It took great effort to raise them to where I could look at them. They were puffed and darkened, pressed hard together in a parody of prayer, bound together by that kind of plastic-covered wire used for extension cords. I raised my hands until I could touch the left side of my head with the back of my right hand. The hand was numb. The pain became more bright and harsh.

"Darling," the small voice said.

I turned my head slowly, experimentally. I saw her on

145

the floor, six feet away, facing me, trussed, foetal, wearing the pinched face of despair. I could see one window spilling that pale light onto the cement floor. Beyond her I could see garden tools, a pump, pressure tanks. To the right of the tanks, between the tanks and the closed door, a man was sprawled face down in deeper shadow, his legs stretched toward me.

"Are——you——all——right?" I asked her in an ancient voice. I spoke from the bottom of a well. Her hair was the palest thing in the room. She wore some sort of dark blue sun suit. Her tender flesh rested against the roughness of the cement floor. The air smelled of damp and rust.

"I'm sorry, I'm sorry," she said and began to cry.

"Where are we?"

"I'm such a damn, damn coward," she whimpered.

"Can you move closer?"

"Yes—I didn't want to. I was afraid I'd . . . find out you were dead." She hitched herself over, writhing, using her heels and elbows. She held herself precariously balanced long enough to kiss me, then burrowed her face into my neck. I felt the heat of her tears on my flesh.

"I found the tracks," she whispered. "Some branches on the bushes were broken. He caught me. Oh, he caught me, Sam."

"Maurice?"

"I'm such a coward. I was going to be full of bright lies and I was going to laugh at him and all that. But he hurt me. God, how he hurt me, Sam! I fainted, and then he hurt me again, terribly, and I couldn't talk fast enough, Sam, telling him all about us. The words just tumbled out, about everything we, we'd guessed. He knows everything now, Sam. I'm so ashamed!"

"Don't be, Peggy. Please don't be. Who is that, over there?"

"Captain Chase. He . . . he's dead, Sam."

"What happened?"

"He . . . he heard me, I think. When I was screaming. I don't think Maurice knew I could scream so loud. He came and . . . there was an argument and they shot him."

"They?"

146

"There's two more men here now, Sam. I think they're the same ones."

"Where are the Mahlers?"

"They sent them away, Sam. In the big car. I don't know where or why."

"It's getting darker. Where is Charity?"

"I haven't seen her since about eleven o'clock this morning. She was drunk then, as bad as I've seen her at that time of day."

"Where is this place . . . in relation to the house?"

"Sort of between the garage and the kitchen."

"How long have we been here?"

"I've been here since . . . about three o'clock. They brought you in a couple of hours later, Sam. Those two men. They didn't put you down. They just sort of . . . dropped you. It was ugly and horrible."

"Has anybody been in here since then?"

"About a half-hour ago the smaller one of the two men came in. I heard the other one call him Marty. He smokes cigars all the time. He was humming to himself, that first part of that old song *Love in Bloom* over and over. He squatted over there and went through Captain Chase's pockets, and then he went over and went through your pockets too. He was a little bit drunk, I think. I asked him if you were dead. All he did was sort of chuckle. Then he came over to me and he . . . put his hands on me. He said filthy things to me and chuckled some more and then he went away. I was crying after he left and calling your name, and moving closer to you little by little and you . . . woke up."

The light was going too quickly. I lifted my hands and looked at the wire on my wrists. It was knotted where I couldn't see the knot. I had her move to a position where she could get her fingers onto the wire around my wrists. I felt the soft weak movements of her fingers.

"Sam, I . . . I can't. There isn't any life in my fingers. It's like when you were little and your hands were half frozen and you couldn't undo buttons."

"Hitch up higher and let me try to use my teeth on yours, honey."

I managed to turn toward her. When I could reach the

147

small hard knot with my mouth, I tried to catch one coil of the knot with my teeth and yank it loose. I would not work.

"Is there anything we can use to cut it?" I asked her.

"It's getting so dark."

"Tools should be over there in the corner. Can you get over there, honey, and see if there's anything?"

"Help me sit up."

I pushed at her clumsily and got her up into a sitting position. She went across the small room by digging her heels against the cement and hiking herself along in a sitting position. It was ludicrous and heartbreaking. I heard a thumping in the darkness, a small metallic claning.

She came hitching back in the same laborious way, breathless with effort. "Will this help? Can we use this, Sam?"

She held it in numb hands against the light, a small triangular metal file.

"If there's any way to hold it, we can use it."

We adjusted our positions so that she was able to hold it between the heels of her numbed hands and, by flexing her elbows, rub it back and forth against the multiple windings of the strands that bound my wrists. I felt a wetness and knew she had gouged the numb flesh.

She stopped and gasped as we heard a blur of male voices beyond the closed door. The file dropped onto my chest.

"Move away from me! Lie down," I whispered.

I could barely see the dark shadow of the file against the paleness of my shirt. I worked at it with my bound wrists, shoving it clumsily inside the front of my shirt, between two buttons. I felt the roughness and relative coolness of it against my skin. I tilted my body and it slid down my ribs on my left side, out of sight.

The door opened. A man some distance away said, "He can carry all that junk, Maurie."

A naked bulb clicked on over the door frame. By the time my eyes had adjusted to the harshness of the light, a sizable man was standing over me. He was swarthy, with black hair, small pouched eyes, a small mustache, too much soft flesh on a heavy bone structure, but still powerful. He kicked me idly, casually, without force, in the left thigh and said, "The smart guy! The big brain."

"Mr. Weber, I presume."

"You presume! Man, you are so right!"

"I think you'd better let us go, Weber. I think that would be the smart thing for you to do."

"I've done a lot of stupid things, Brice. So it got me in a big mess. Now I get out of it. I should have dropped Charlie-boy into the Gulf over two years ago. But there wasn't time to get anybody to help me, and she got right down on her knees and begged, so what the hell. It would have saved a lot of trouble. You would have lived a lot longer."

"What was he after? What was in your safe?"

"You're so smart and you don't even know that?"

"I know what I think it was. I think it was . . . is, something you're holding over Charity."

"Just a couple of pieces of paper, Brice. And a couple of pictures, and a little reel of tape, all wrapped for mailing. All the time its been like having the next twenty years of her life all wrapped up, because that's the least she could expect if I ever mailed them."

"The murder of her second husband?"

"Let's just say she helped arrange it."

"But you never married her, Weber?"

"Christ, no!"

"So she's been part of the deal?"

"You tell me what kind of a deal, friend."

I knew I shouldn't keep on with it. I was showing off, and it wasn't helping either of us. "Haven't you been living the big dream, Weber? Living way over your head? I don't know how you put the squeeze on, or who you put it on, but you got just what you asked for. House and boat and a hunk of cash once a month and servants and exactly the kind of woman a man like you would want to own."

"It's nice to own a woman this way, Brice. You don't have to beat on her at all. Not when you've got the pressure locked up in a safe."

"So somebody set up Starr Development to keep you happy. Did it turn out to be everything you ever wanted?"

149

"I've been living as good as a man can live, Brice. What more do you need? And it's going to keep on just the same way."

"Why did Charlie take his medicine like a little man?"

He kicked me again, with more emphasis. "I got careless about keeping that broad close to home. I even let her talk me into getting a car for her. So she went after that kid, and she put out for him, and snowed him so bad he was ready to do anything for her, like cracking a safe, but I caught him. She was tired of being owned, I guess. But I told him the story he would tell, and I had a gun that couldn't be traced to plant on him, and I told him that if he didn't plead guilty I was going to kill his brand new girl friend, and I told him just exactly how I was going to do it, and how long it was going to take. And she was there to back me up, and plead with him too, because she damn well know I would do it. So it took over two years of doing hard time before she wore off him enough so he could start thinking again, instead of just remembering how good she was at it and how noble he was to save her from being killed."

"What did he think was in the safe?"

"God knows what she told him. I never asked. But it would have had to be lies, and when I heard he'd escaped, I figured he'd come back to find out just how much of it was lies. Jail can tough up a soft kid, so I figured some help would be nice to have around. It came in handy, Brice."

"And they never went back?"

"They were ordered to hang around Tampa for a couple of weeks to see if things died down okay."

"But they didn't."

"They will now, Brice. They will now."

"That's a pretty good trick, but I don't think you can do it."

"Don't you?"

"There's too much you're going to have to explain, Weber."

"Maybe by the time anybody gets around to asking me anything, I won't be here any more."

"They'll find you." I didn't sound very convincing.

"You're the big brain, Brice, going around figuring everything out. See if you can pick any holes in this situation. Charity is aboard the *Sea Queen*, dead drunk. After she passed out, I poured a little more into her. She doesn't know what the hell has been going on all day."

"So what?"

"She doesn't even know that today I phoned that nice friendly sheriff you got here and I told him . . . I mean I *asked* him if it was okay if we went on a cruise, around to the east coast. I said we thought we'd try living on the boat for a while, at Lauderdale, at that Bahia Mar place. I said he could get hold of us there if he had any questions about anything. I said you and my sister-in-law were coming for the ride. He told me I wasn't very choosy about who I asked onto my boat."

"There are other people who will know I wouldn't . . ."

"Wait until you get the whole picture, friend. Your wagon is back at that cottage of yours, parked and locked, and there's a note stuck to your door and printed on it is the message, 'Back in a week.' I had the Mahlers pack up and take off to drive the car over to Lauderdale and find a place to stay so they'll be there to meet the happy cruise folk. The rental car is in the drive. Ben is going to take it down to Naples. You and me and Marty and the two gals and our deceased captain are all leaving aboard the *Sea Queen* inside the hour. We'll be towing the dingy with the outboard on her. Once we get outside and get on course, I'll set the automatic pilot and Marty and me can have some fun with this little sister here. But when we get off Naples, the party will be over. We'll make you all comfortable, open the sea cocks and take off in the dingy. Once we get ashore we'll push that loose too. It will be one of the mysteries of the sea, buddy. My personal stuff is in the car. By tomorrow night we'll be three ordinary guys, flying north. It'll be a week before the excitement starts. And that's more than enough time."

I moved my lashed hands, and, looking down at them, saw the small coppery glintings where the edge of the file had cut through the plastic insulation. I moved them to a position where he would be less likely to notice these marks.

"Pick a hole in it, friend?"

"They'll be looking for you."

"If they decide I wasn't lost at sea with the rest of the people."

"You haven't told me all of it. You haven't told me why."

"Why?"

"Or how. Or who are you. The name isn't Maurice Weber, is it?"

"The Maurie is straight. Not the Weber."

"A city hall type. It shows on you, Maurie. A crummy little political leech who spent most of his life trying to pretend he was important. Ignorant, stupid, greedy and dangerous. You've got the manner, boy. How did you start out? Running errands for the boss of your ward."

He kicked me in the waist, in the left side. The pain made me gasp.

"They *thought* I was stupid," he said in a thickened voice. "They give me the big payoff for loyalty, a crummy job in the assessor's office. Sixty-fi' lousy bucks a week. They thought I was so loyal and so stupid, I was the guy to trust with their fat payoffs. They'd slip me an extra ten. Big deal! So after I got smart I kept on acting stupid, just like before. But I was checking out every deal, every payoff. I got me one of those little cameras and I learned how to use it. I packed a transistor tape recorder around. I kept a day by day record. For three years I worked, nailing them all down, all the big names, all the fat cats. I knew the union payoffs and the construction kickbacks and all the ways the grease filtered upstream from the beat cops to the boys on top. I made three complete sets of everything and I planted two of them in the safest places in the world, where if I didn't check in four times a year, the packages would be sent direct to the F.B.I., which is about the only deal those boys can't fix. The Special Grand Jury was in session and I gave them an anonymous tip to call me in. The D.A. was fixed and he let the big boys know about it and it made them nervous so they called me in. Papers had already been served on me. So I turned over one complete package. You should have seen their faces. Stupid, loyal Maurie. I laid it right on the line. I told them just what I wanted. A house like this, a yacht, servants, a chunk of cash twelve times a year and some gorgeous broad who'd do anything I told her to. They set it up through a dummy corporation, the house and yacht and so forth, to keep the tax boys off me. I had to pick a new name on account of a warrant being issued when I didn't show. And it would still be going on if I hadn't made two mistakes. I shouldn't have gone so soft she got a chance to mess with that Charlie-boy. And I shouldn't have let her ask little sister down here. But it's nothing that can't be cured. It can all be cured overnight."

"Where did you get the two assistant assassins, Maurie?"

He shrugged. "The boys I put the squeeze on, they're prominent citizens, but the way they operate, they got mob connections. They have to have. So I got the loan of a couple of specialists."

"Do your previous employers approve of your . . . killing people?"

"All they care about is to stay the hell out of prison, and that's where they all go if anything bad happens to me. They're big men. They would hate to give up the big cars and the fancy women and the club memberships."

"Why did you kill the girl too?"

"Because she was with Charlie-boy. There wasn't any choice."

"Did they come here?"

"Together, right to the door, Brice. The girl called Char, and she told them she was alone in the house. They walked right into it. I've got to see how things are coming along."

He walked out into the night, leaving the light on.

"Horrible, horrible," Peggy whispered. She moved near me and I was just telling her where the file was when Weber came back with the two men. The smaller of the two wore a cigar and the yachting cap I had last seen on Stan Chase. He had the face of a fat sleepy weasel. The other one, the one Maurie had called Ben, was bigger than I am, with a bulging redness of freckled face, surprised blue eyes and a carroty brush cut.

"Put her in one of the bunks," Weber ordered.

"A pleasure," the weasel said. "Open wide, sweets." She would not open her mouth until they worked hard thumbs

153

JOHN D. MAC DONALD

against the corners of her jaw. When her mouth gaped the weasel crammed a blue plastic sponge into it and tied it in place with a length of clothesline. She made thin gagging sounds as they started to carry her out. The big one mumbled something to the weasel, then took her in his big arms and carried her out effortlessly.

Maurie and the weasel removed Chase's body, carrying him with Maurie's fingers laced across Chase's chest, the weasel carrying him by the ankles. I was left alone for perhaps ten minutes.

Ten minutes can be long, long, long. Bitter, black and long. In one corner of my mind I could applaud the bold planning of Weber. He had made some mistakes, endangering the lush life he had promoted for himself. After having been thought stupid for so long, he found it gratifying to think of the monumental stupidity of the rest of the human race. (I was trying to work the file out of its hiding place so that I might try to put it to some clumsy use.)

Out of arrogance he had made mistakes. He had thought himself bright enough to kill and get away with it. Now he accepted the fact that the job had been so slipshod he would have to give up his corner of paradise. He was taking his loss. Once he was free and clear, he still had his hand on the money machine.

I could sense how the men he had so carefully blackmailed thought of him. They had made a tactical mistake. He had wrapped them up neatly. And so their only possible course of action had been to give him exactly what he wanted, and wish him a long life. His support had become a matter of business insurance, and very probably a minor expense item compared with the size of the gross. If they were wise they would be delighted that they had not been blackmailed by a man anxious for power and position within their organizational structure. Actually the outlay was minor. The land, house and cruiser were owned by Starr Development, presupposing an eventual liquidation which would return most of the capital involved. The cash payment each month would certainly be no more than two thousand dollars, a tiny part of the illegal gross in any corrupt municipality of any size.

He had trapped them into financing the kind of life he wanted to lead, and they could rejoice that his wants—in comparison to his leverage—were simple.

I could even be so objective as to see an untidy parallel between his chosen life and mine. Each in our own way, we had stepped out of the arena. Were his motives any less valid than mine?

With a continuing exercise of objectivity, I could see just how it would all come out. It was Sunday evening, one week since Charlie had stood outside my bedroom window in the wind. It would be perhaps as long as another week before the *Sea Queen* was reported missing. The Coast Guard would mount an air search. I could, through an exercise of optimism, assume that a few people would raise enough hell to compel a thorough investigation. D. Ackley Bush, J.B., possibly Peggy's people, Jaimie France. Through some bright newspaper people the world might be made aware of the odd fact of there being too many disappearances.

I could guess that Lou Leeman would leap into the act, thus focusing attention on Starr Development. But if it had been set up with enough care, it would be impossible to check it back through the dummies involved to the actual principals And if, much too late, anybody did get onto the lead of the rental car, it would be impossible to trace Weber. He would have escaped, with his leverage intact, able to safely demand a new paradise and a new captive woman, in Arizona, California or one of the islands of the Carribean. In any city on any day you see forty men who look enough like Weber to be his brother. For the man without resources, a new identity is difficult to assume. Weber could safely demand everything he needed. (I tried to grasp the edge of the file with my fingers, but I could not even know if my fingers responded to the orders of the brain.)

Rage is an empty weapon. Terror only makes a man more helpless. My terror was for her, not for myself. Her death would be the unforgivable waste. I struggled to keep the raw flood of emotion out of my mind. I hoped that I might be given some small chance before it all ended, and if I were to be capable of taking the maximum

155

advantage of any small chance, I would have to remain as cold as an assassin, as impersonal as a weapon. Emotion could even blind me to the small chance so that I would never become aware of it. If I was given no chance to function, or missed the chance because I was beyond any exercise of logic, I would spend eternity with my beloved in a coffin of teak, mahogany and bronze on the floor of the shallow Gulf of Mexico.

When you have suddenly begun to return to life, death becomes a more bitter irony, more heartbreaking. (I lost the file and turned my body cautiously and discovered it had slipped back down between my shirt and my ribs.)

In tribute to the size of me, the three of them came back after me. They packed my mouth with a greasy rag and tied it in place. Weber hugged my bound ankles against his side. Marty and Ben each took me by an upper arm. They dropped me in the night grass while Weber turned out the light, closed the utility room door, snapped a padlock in place.

It was the calmest of nights. I could hear faraway trucks on the mainland highway. An airliner went over, running lights blinking steadily. People sat quietly up there, eight thousand feet over the dark tropic land, and perhaps the hostesses were stowing the soiled dishes from the evening meal.

They carried me aboard the Sea Queen and dropped me onto the teak deck near the stern. I tried to hold my neck rigid to keep my head from hitting, but it snapped back and hit hard enough to daze me for a few moments. The previous blow on the head and the taste of gasoline on the rag nauseated me. I fought it, suspecting I might strangle if I became actively sick. The peak of nausea slowly subsided.

Ben and Weber walked up the dark lawn toward the house. Marty sat with one haunch on the rail. I heard him spit the bitten end of a new cigar into the bay water, and saw the pulsing glow of the flame on his fatty weasel face as he lighted the cigar. I lay across the rear cockpit deck, my head to starboard. The waning moon was beginning to rise above the mainland. I rolled my head in a gingerly way to the left, looking toward the stern, and saw the body of Chase sprawled close beside me, on its back, the face like wax in the first touch of moonlight, mouth agape, the one eye I could see half open, but without that wet glitter of life. Dead eyes soon take on a dusty look and reflect no light.

I heard a car start up nearby, and soon head north up the Key, the motor sound fading into the night silence.

Weber came onto the dock. Marty spoke in the low voice of conspiracy. "All set now?"

"He'll be waiting in the parking lot next to the big city pier they got down there."

"He's got my stuff too?"

"You put it in the car yourself, didn't you? What do you think we did? Throw it the hell out? The house is locked, the electric turned off, the safe is empty. You worry too much, Marty."

"God damn well told, I worry! I told you last week, you do things too fancy, it just means that many more things go wrong. You thought it was so cute, dumping that little car in the water, and we bust our ass getting it onto the boat and it didn't turn out so cute after all, pal."

I watched Weber stand and look at the man for long moments.

"What were your orders, Marty?"

"My orders? I guess my orders were to take orders from you, Maurie, but I know more about the rough stuff than you do. Right?"

"Sure, Marty. They can give you a name and description and send you to some city where you've never been, and you can blow a man in half in his own driveway and get away clean. That's nice. So give me the benefit of your expert advice, Marty. Shall we leave these people in the driveway, maybe? How else do we hide four bodies where they'll never be found, and have them figure me for missing, presumed dead? Give me a better plan, Marty."

There was another silence. Marty finally said, "So let's go for a boat ride."

Chapter Ten

By THE TIME we had moved out into the channel in the bay, I knew Weber had watched Chase often enough so that he had learned to do it by the book. The running lights were on. The dingy was riding on the tow line the proper distance astern. The two diesels were running in sync at, I guessed, about a thousand r.p.m. Weber, with Marty beside him, was operating the Sea Queen from the flying bridge, hand operating the big spotlight to pick up the reflectors on the channel markers.

I knew when we made the turn to starboard and went out through Horseshoe Pass. I knew the tide was a little past the high, and I was praying for Weber to run aground on one of the shifting bars, but he moved with care and deliberation. There was enough swell outside the pass, beyond the bars, to give the Sea Queen a different motion. When he put on more throttle I knew we were clear.

They came down the narrow curving ladderway from the flying bridge and Weber went to the duplicate controls in the semi-enclosed bridge a dozen feet from me. He turned on the chart light.

They spoke over the deep purring of the diesels, raising their voices just enough so I could hear them.

"Now what are you doing?" Marty demanded.

"We'll run straight out a couple of miles, then take a compass heading that will take us down to Naples."

"How do you know it will?"

"Because, goddammit, Chase put all the compensated compass headings on this here chart and I'm reading the right one, goddammit!"

158

"So don't get sore. I'm just asking."

Weber gave the craft a little more throttle, then came astern with a flashlight, stepping over me and over the body as though we didn't exist, to check how the dingy was riding.

When he went back to the controls Marty said, "We got gas enough?"

"Yes, we've got gas enough."

"I just don't want anything should go wrong, Maurie."

"For God's sake!"

"I get uneasy about all this water."

Weber didn't answer.

"After you open up the bottom like you said, Maurie, how long will it take it to sink?"

"Twenty minutes to a half-hour."

"It will really sink?"

"Like a stone."

"How far out will it sink?"

"I don't know! We'll get you into the dingy and all set. I'll get it headed straight out on automatic pilot and give it full throttle and go over the side. You'll have my clothes in the dingy. She may go five miles before the water shorts out the power. And I've told you this three times already."

"How about the people?"

"You're the expert. You get to knock them out. Then we'll unwire Brice and little sister. We'll stow everybody below. If they're ever found, it'll show they drowned."

"Except the guy Ben shot."

"That will be one of the mysteries of the sea."

"What are you doing now, Maurie?"

"We're far enough out. I got to put it on course."

I felt the change of direction.

"What's that thing?"

"I'm throwing it over onto automatic pilot."

"Hey, that's pretty spooky, that wheel moving back and forth all by itself."

"I missed it by a couple of degrees. Got to try again."

I heard the thud again as the automatic pilot was engaged.

After a few moments Weber said, "There! That'll do."

"When do we get where we're going?"

"What did I tell Ben?"

"You said about two o'clock."

"Well?"

"Jesus Christ, Maurie, can't I even talk? How will we know when we're there?"

"From the lights of the city, stupid."

"I will be one happy son of a bitch when this is over," Marty said dolefully.

"Now we can go below and get a drink."

"Doesn't somebody have to look out in front there in case we're going to run into something?"

"The only thing we can run into is another boat, Marty. All boats have running lights. It's a clear night. Now look out there. Way out. See that light?"

"Sure, what is . . ."

"Another boat, running way out, maybe eight miles off shore. The only thing we could hit would be another boat running on automatic so there'd be nobody at the wheel, and this is a hell of a lot of empty space to be on a collision course by accident. If it will make you feel better, we'll take a look every twenty minutes or so."

"I don't like this running along blind in the dark, Maurie, honest to God."

"So let's get a drink and take your mind off it, and let's play some games with the little sister."

"But not like with that big broad—we didn't know her name was Sis until after."

"You didn't like it?"

"How could I like it? By the time it's my turn, I thought she was dead."

"She wasn't."

"Okay, so she wasn't. But by then who could tell? There's got to be some type reaction."

"You want reaction, we'll give you some, Marty. Maybe you'll get more than you want. Maybe, like Ben, you ought to settle for Charity."

As they went below I heard Marty make a sound of righteous disgust. "Me, I could never stand a drunk woman. Honest to God. It goes against me somehow."

More lights went on in the main lounge. The light

160

shone out across the deck, dwindling the weak moonlight. I could hear the constant roar of the water as the displacement hull thrust it aside. It closed in behind us, in foam and turmoil. I began to work once again to get at the file. I had the idea that I might be able to wedge it upright between the boards of the teak deck. But when I rolled, I felt it slip around to the small of my back.

I fumbled weakly at my shirt and managed to pull it out in front, but I could not get the back of it free.

Suddenly, over all the sound of the marine engines and the rushing of the sea, I heard a thin climbing wail, a prolonged ululation from the captive throat of my girl. Without words, it expressed outrage and a dreadful panic with such clarity that my own breathing stopped and the sweat on my body was suddenly icy. They had either taken the gag from her mouth, or it had been displaced in struggle. I heard a male roar of anger, and I heard Weber's heavy phlegmy laughter, and then I heard her making a curious yelping sound.

I was suddenly far beyond careful thoughts, cool planning. Desperation can create a kind of madness, an insane energy. I was on my right side. The wire kept the heels of my hands firmly pressed together, and the wire went far enough up my wrists so as to keep my elbows tucked against my sides. I shut my eyes and forced my elbows out. I could feel the muscles of arms and shoulders bulge like marble against my skin. Vermilion dots swarmed in the blackness behind my eyes. I canted my head onto my shoulder in strain, lips pulled back away from my teeth, my lungs full to bursting, my throat closed. Something would give. It could be bone that would crack, or muscle fiber that would rip away, or the wire that would break. I know the pain must have been great, but I had no awareness of pain. It was an autohypnosis created by an extremity of effort.

Suddenly there was a small popping sound, absurdly tiny to be the product of the most concentrated strain I have ever experienced. I sensed rather than felt a sliding and loosening at my wrists. I opened my eyes and moved them into the path of light from the main cabin. The wire had parted, probably where she had begun to cut into the copper core with the small file. I quickly worked the encircling strands loose. (She screamed in torment and anger.)

My hands were free. I reached down to my ankles. I could feel the senseless fingers fumbling weakly and ineffectually at my ankles. I forced myself into a sitting position and slammed my hands against the teak deck to force some life into them. As life began to seep back into the numbness of swollen tissue the pain was electric and violent. I knew it would be a long time before they regained enough deftness to deal with knotted wire. I groped for the file and I was able to close my hand around it, the way an infant holds a spoon.

("Bastards!" she yelled at the top of her lungs. "Bastards, bastards, bastards!")

I swung my ankles into the light and sawed feebly at the exposed wire. It parted after an anguished eternity, and after I had unwrapped the wire I yanked the length of clothesline loose and pulled the sickening cloth out of my mouth. I tried to stand and went sprawling. Both feet were numb. I pulled myself up and stood, holding onto the rail, stamping my feet, trying to bring the feeling back into them.

("Stop!" she screamed. "Oh God! Stop!")

I tested my weight on feet that felt like wooden paddles. My hands hung like sacks of putty. I tried to move fast, hoping for surprise, knowing I had no time left.

I went stumbling, lurching down into the brightness of the big lounge. The three of them were at a low divan at my left. Weber was at the far end of the couch, kneeling, laughing, holding her shoulders down. He was facing me. Peggy's wrists were still bound. She was naked. She was writhing, thrashing spasming her torso and her lean strong legs. Marty, naked except for his shirt, was cursing, struggling, trying to pin and separate her legs so as to consumate this tethered rape. His back was to me.

As Weber saw me, his eyes went wide. He released her and sprang back.

"Hold her!" Marty yelled in fury.

I reached him in two lurching strides. I could not

162

make fists and so I chopped down on the nape of his neck with the underside of my right forearm. As he dropped, limp and sighing, Peggy rolled off the couch and up onto her feet, her face wild and vacant, looking at me and through me with no recognition.

"Run!" I yelled into her face. "Go over the side!"

I knew what Weber was going after, with great speed and direction. I knew I could not stop him, could not even reach him in time. I slapped her face with my flaccid hand. Her eyes seemed to focus. "Over the side!" I yelled once more. She slid fleetly by me. I followed her, blundering, off balance, going too slowly, like one of those nightmares when, in panic, you run from some monstrous Thing, and it is like running through glue.

As I started to pull myself out onto the deck I heard the hard flat bark of the shot. My hand stung where I grasped the edge of the hatch, and tiny things bit into my cheek and throat. I stumbled out onto the deck, veering to my right to evade the line of fire, and I saw her going over the stern. Panic had made her run straight back to dive over the stern rail. I saw her stretched sleek and pale in the moonlight, and I knew that if she entered the water in that sort of dive, the layers of turbulence behind the cruiser would snap her back and her neck and break her legs, if she did not land in the dingy. But just before she fell away into the darkness I saw her curl herself into a ball.

I went over the port rail, hurling myself as far as I could. I smacked the water hard and went far under, wrenched and twisted, spinning, hearing the hard underwater chunking sound of the twin screws. When the water was more quiet I swam under water for as far as I could, hoping I was swimming away from the boat. I came up. The Sea Queen was twice as far away from me as I had dared hope.

I looked for Peggy. She was expert enough to handle herself in the water with bound hands. I knew she had jumped far enough to be clear of the screws. I looked along a path of moonlight. It was empty.

"Peggy!" I yelled her name and listened.

"Peggy!" I listened to too much silence and heard a

faint reply. I swam in that direction for fifty yards.

"Peggy!"

"Sam," she called. "Sam."

I saw her forty feet away and swam to her.

"Sam, they were trying to . . ."

"I know. Snap out of it. We've got to be smart, honey. We're going to have to spend a lot of time underwater."

"I can't stay under with my hands . . ."

"I know. So I'll have to pull you down and try to keep you down. Here they come."

The *Sea Queen*, back under manual steering, had finally circled back to search along the path. She came on fast and I could see the white water at her bow. I knew Weber would be up on the flying bridge. Once I could see which way he would pass us—on which side— I set about increasing the distance there would be between us. I slipped my right arm through her arms and slipped her bound hands up over my shoulder so I could tow her and still use both arms. She kicked with reassuring strength and we moved a little faster than I had hoped. When he was so close I was afraid he could detect movement in the moonlit water, we rested.

I said in a low voice, "Be ready to go under. He'll use that damn searchlight."

As I had hoped, he stopped short of where we had gone over the side. It is easy to underestimate distance and momentum on the water. He braked it by reversing both engines and then seemed to lay dead in the water. I put my head under to check, and I could not hear any slow churning of the twin screws.

He lay a hundred yards away. The running lights suddenly went off. There was silence. The big white beam came on suddenly. He began to work it back and forth in a random pattern. When it started to come close I said, "Dive." We went down. The water was as warm as soup. It had a stubborn buoyancy that made me fight hard to keep us under. At last I had to surface. They were shining the big light on the water on the far side of the boat.

"They could have drowned easy," Marty said. It was startling the way his voice carried over the water.

"Shut up!"

164

"Look, her hands are wired together, right? And you think you got him in the air on that second shot. So why shouldn't they drown?"

"You were such big help."

"It was Ben put the wire on him, not me, pal. He come up behind me and hit me a good one. How far is the shore?"

"Maybe four miles."

"How long can you keep shining that light around before somebody sees it and thinks maybe it's a boat in distress and reports it, Maurie?"

"I think that light way back there is Boca Grande, Marty. So we're maybe seven miles south of there, and this is empty country."

"I still don't like it. I told you something would go wrong, dint I?"

"For Chrissake, shut up!"

"Amateurs always get too damn fancy."

"You get on the light. I'm going to make some big circles around here and keep looking."

I heard the engines go into gear. He started making his first circle, going much too fast for an effective search. I guessed he was losing his temper and his patience. I could predict the path of the cruiser, but not the crazy pattern of the light. I was afraid he would blunder onto us. His second circle carried him dangerously close, and we went under when he went by. His third circle swung out around us, and after we were under, I saw the water all around us lighted up by the searchlight beam.

When I came up, Peggy was coughing and retching. "I . . . swallowed some," she said. "You stayed under so long."

She barely had time to recover before he came around again, and it seemed as if he would run us down. I waited as long as I dared and saw the bow swing slightly, so when I went down I tried to move in the opposite direction. When the turbulence caught us and rolled us, I knew how close it had been.

That was the last time he came anywhere near us. We floated and watched. He was two hundred yards, five hundred yards, and then a mile away.

"Darling, darling," she said.

"There is one last thing I want to see," I told her. And then I saw it. The running lights came on. He straightened away on course, running south, leaving us in the bland emptiness of the sea.

"We're so far out, darling," she said.

"Just a little swim on a hot night. Refreshing."

"But which way do we go?"

"We go that way until we walk up onto dry land, girl. It should be LaCosta Key."

"Can you undo my hands, darling?"

I tried. My fingers were still like breadsticks. "Later, maybe. I'll try again later, honey."

"But I can't help us at all. It will all be up to you."

"You can help us a little."

I had been able to kick my shoes off shortly after jumping off the boat. My pockets were empty. The shirt and slacks were light weight. I was tempted to shed them until I realized they might be very useful when we reached shore.

Had I been alone, I could have paced myself and had no trouble. You swim until you feel as if your arms are turning to lead, and then you float for a while, and start off again, using a different stroke.

There weren't enough ways I could haul her along and make any kind of time. The best way was to have her behind me, holding onto my belt, floating along between my legs, adding her kicking to my lumbering crawl stroke. But I could not keep that up very long. We would rest and then shift so that I did a back stroke with Peggy clinging to one ankle, being towed along, helping us with her kicking. Our least effective method was when I hooked her clasped hands over my shoulder and did a side stroke.

In water less warm and less buoyant, we could not have made it. And for a long time I doubted whether we could make it even under these most favorable conditions. Water is an alien element. It saps strength. It became a blind feat of endurance. Each time I tired more quickly.

After a long, long time I realized she was speaking my name. I rolled onto my back, gasping, trying to will the tensions out of my muscles which made it difficult to float.

"You go on and get help," she said. "I can float around for days, happy as a clam, really."

When I could speak I said, "Nonsense. I'm enjoying every minute."

"My God, aren't we bright and brittle and gay," she said, her voice breaking. "We'll make our crummy little quips right to the end, won't we?"

"Hey," I said. "Don't!"

"Well, I'm sick of gallantry, Sam. I love you with all my heart. Leave me right here. Swim to shore."

"Quips or no quips, Peggy, I'll never leave you. We'll make it together or we won't make it."

"Then we won't make it, Sam. You were groaning with every breath."

"I'll rest a little. Then I'll be okay."

"How far are we from shore?"

"Half way, at least."

"If it ends like this, it's such . . . a dirty cheat."

"It won't. Believe me, it won't!"

"Don't kid me, Sam. I'm a big girl."

We floated in the darkness and the silence. I added it all up, and there was only one way in the world I could make it come out right.

"I better see what I can do with that knot again, honey."

"That's the way I figured it out too. Darling?"

"What?"

"Good luck."

I found the knot in the darkness and the short ends of wire. My fingers had more feeling, but they were still clumsy. I was exhausted and the effort kept pushing me underwater. I pawed at the knot and gnawed it and suddenly I had to rest.

"Are you getting anywhere?" she asked, too calm.

"I'm pretty sure I am," I lied.

"If you can't do it, I'll make you leave me. I'll move away from you, Sam. You won't find me in the dark. I won't answer you."

"Stop that! Stop that stupid goddam nonsense!"

I tried again until I was exhausted, but I kept my hand on her wrist while I floated and rested. On the third attempt I went underwater, and got a dog tooth wedged in a loop of the knot, felt the edge of wire gash my gum, yanked my head like a wolf tearing meat, and felt the miraculous loosening.

Moments later the wire was on the floor of the Gulf, and she was sobbing and laughing, glorious in that moonlight.

Then she swam slowly around me, working the circulation back into her hands. She came to me, pressed salt lips against mine and said, "Race you to shore, mister?"

"More quips?"

"Now it's different, darling. We can afford them."

"I have the feeling you'll win."

"Tell me when you're ready to start."

"Right now, but slow."

"Make the pace, Sam."

We swam side by side. She adjusted her pace to mine. I thought it would be a lot easier without her, but I soon learned I had expended almost everything in the account. There was very little left. If I didn't husband it with great care, I would not make it.

She was calling to me again and she came over and caught my arm, stopping me. I felt like crying childish tears because somebody had stopped me and I didn't know if I could get going again, ever.

"Sam," she said. "Look, darling."

I looked. I saw the darkness of the shoreline.

I found I could start my arms moving again. And after a long time my knee touched bottom. I staggered up onto my feet and fell forward, and tried to get up again and could not. I was crawling onto wet sand when she caught my arm and helped me up. I leaned too much of my weight on her as we plodded up to where the sand was dry and still warm with the lingering heat of the sun that was long gone. I slid down onto my knees and rolled over onto my back, chest heaving, heart laboring. She knelt beside me and sat back on her heels.

After a long time I was able to look at her. She was mostly a shadow that blotted out the stars. But the moonlight made her hair bright, and it came down at an oblique angle, touching her here and there with a faint silver wash. It touched her cheek, the tip of her nose, her shoulder, half of one breast and the tip of the other, a faint curve of hip, a bold roundness of flexed thigh. The Gulf lapped at the sand, tame as a puppy.

"Old hero type," my girl said softly. "Stubborn, durable, and so forth."

"It ain't often I take a moonlight swim with a naked gal."

"I'm being sweet to you because I'm actually after your shirt." She moved to spread herself sweetly across my chest and kiss the side of my throat and nestle there. I ran my hand along the firm satin of her back.

"Everything from now on," she whispered, "is all profit."

"All for free, honey."

"How did you get loose?"

"When you were screaming it turned out I was able to bust that wire. I think it broke where you weakened it with the file."

She shuddered against me. "They took that nasty sponge out of my mouth because that Marty one wanted me to scream. I was hoping to get a chance to bite him."

"Did he manage to . . ."

"No, darling. But let's just say that it couldn't have been timed any closer. He'd clubbed me over the ear with his fist and I was fighting in a sort of daze. It wasn't going to take him much longer. Hey, do you know that I loooove you?"

"What you feel is gratitude, woman."

There was a small multiple whining that kept increasing in its ominous volume. My girl began to twitch. She sat up. "Sam, there's a hundred billion mosquitoes here! We're going to get eaten alive!"

"Lucky thing a tourist like you has a native along."

I sent her out into the water. I stripped down to my shorts, wrung out the shirt and trousers and spread them on driftwood sticks stuck into the sand. And then I joined her in the shallows. When too many of them started to swarm around our faces, we would duck under and move away from them. As my strength returned there came with it a special urgency of desire for her. Any nearness of death seems to quicken the needs of the body. The warm and shallow water and the faint almost imperceptible swell and the moonlight, making the beach sand into snow, had aphrodisiac qualities, and she was creamy and supple beside me, with a gaiety that had a semi-hysterical quality about it, a gayety marked by constant awareness of the narrow margin of our escape.

It started as a kind of love play, with both of us knowing that this was not the time or the place, both of us aware of a leaden weariness. For a little time our play seemed to have the innocence of children, little wrestlings and graspings and mock angers. But soon she was responding in drugged and humid ways. The shorts floated off in the black water. I took her, there, in the warm shallows, her drenched and shining head resting at that line where the ripples of the outgoing tide touched the beach, the greedy insects, ignored for a time, feeding thick and fat on my back and shoulders and on the careless arch of her long legs, our joined bodies buoyant in that shallow edge of the tropic sea.

After it ended, the greedy keening of thousands of tiny wings sent us back into deeper water.

She clung to me with a desperate strength and with all of her wrapped around me, she whispered fiercely in my ear, "Don't ever be sorry. Don't ever be sorry we started just this way."

"There couldn't be any other way to start. You know that."

"It was glorious! That's a big word, but there it is. Glorious."

"You don't have to say it like a challenge."

Soon she began to get a little sleepy and cross and wanted to know if she was expected to sleep in the darn water. I went up and felt the shirt and trousers for the third time and found them dry enough. I hastily scooped two long holes up in the clean, dry, warm sand. I had her come running and stretch out with her head on her sand pillow, and I covered her over with a layer of sand, then propped the sport shirt on four sticks so that it substituted for mosquito netting over her head. I was thoroughly bitten before I had made the same arrangements beside her, for myself, breathing through the propped-up mesh of the tropical weight slacks.

"Good night, my darling," she said in a very crisp and matter-of-fact voice. A few minutes later when I asked her if she could get to sleep, there was no answer.

When the early sun woke me up I sat up to find her nest empty. It was a morning full of sparkle and glints of light, a west wind.

"Hoo!" she cried from a hundred yards out. "Hallooo!"

I stood up out of the sand. I walked down to the edge of the water. Every muscle was full of broken dishes and fish hooks. I was a hundred and nine years old. I swam slowly out to her.

"Good morning, my love," she said. "My hair is a gummy horrible mess. I didn't bring my lipstick. I'm red welts all over from bugs. I've got little gray balloons under my eyes, I think. Take a good look. And then, if you could bear it, kiss a girl good morning."

I did. I said, "The looks are nifty. It's the good cheer I can't stand."

"Come on and swim out a little further. I want to show you something."

I churned along in her wake and then she turned and pointed back. I saw it too, a tall white water tower shining against the deepening blue of the morning sky.

"Civilization?" she asked.

"I don't know how far south we are from Boca. This could be LaCosta Key, and that would be the tower on one of the islands in Pine Island Sound."

"Darling, I know we should be grimly determined to get to a phone and confound the evil ones and all that, but I want to stay. Am I perverse? If there was any coffee, you couldn't make me leave."

"We'll come back."

"For sure? In the *Lesser Evil*? Is that a promise?"

"Solemn. Cross my . . ." I stopped as I saw her hand. I caught her wrist as she tried to snatch it away. I looked at the angry, puffy redness on the back of her hand, the places newly scabbed.

"What did this?"

"It doesn't hurt now, really."

"It's what made you talk?"

"Yes."

"Cigarettes?"

"That damned cigar."

"Six places, Peggy. Six bad burns."

171

"The box score goes like this, darling. I lasted through four, somehow, fainted on the fifth, and talked like mad on the sixth."

"And called yourself a coward?"

"For talking at all, Sam. My God, I didn't wait for questions. I was volunteering information. I told them everything we'd guessed about them."

I touched the back of her hand with my lips. And because I felt a warning sting in my eyes, I ducked her firmly and headed for shore at my very best pace, stretching the hot little wires interlaced through my muscles. The swim was loosening me up a little. Twenty feet from shore she started to boil past me, but she was too close, so I reached out and caught one arm, pulled her back and ducked her again, and got to shore first.

I walked up and pulled the slacks on.

"You're a lousy cheater!" she yelled. I turned and beamed at her. She lay in shallow water with her head out. "Bring me my shirt!"

"Come on up here and ask pleasantly and politely if you may borrow my shirt, woman, and I'll decide whether to let you have it."

"Sam!"

"Take your time, cutie."

She scowled at me, and then finally stood up in the shallows. She tried to screen herself with arms and hands, and then said, "Oh, the heck with it." She combed her soaked hair back with her fingers, squared her shoulders and came toward me, up the twenty-foot slant of beach, shyly at first and then with an increasing pride and boldness.

She walked in the brightness of the morning sun, with the sea bright and blue behind her, the droplets of water spangling her body, taut with grace and balance, her head a little to one side, her expression solemn, her eyes fixed on mine. She marched up to me, took a deep breath that lifted breasts that were small, tilted and perfect.

"What is entirely and forever yours, Sam, you have every right to look at," she said. "Anything less than that would be silly."

Entirely and forever mine. It came thundering in upon me, this absolute and total emotional responsibility. I gladly accepted it. But I knew it was something that was happening to me for the very first time. Until that moment I had always been alone . . . even in the days of Judy. Even last night, with Peggy, I had been a little bit apart from her and from everyone else in the world. But with that special tone of voice and the look in her eyes she had pried open the last crypt, letting the stale cold air out, filling that final corner of me with a warmth I had never known before.

"Aren't—you supposed to say something sort of nice?" she asked in a small voice.

"You are the most beautiful woman in the world."

"Not *that* nice!"

"It's all complete and total and forever."

"Tell me that once a day for a long, long time, Sam. Please. And now maybe you'd let go of that shirt?"

She put it on and buttoned it. The shoulder seams drooped halfway to her elbows. Her wrists, like mine, were still grooved, bruised and swollen. The bottom of the sport shirt would have hung sedately to mid thigh, but the west wind kept plucking at it, lifting it.

She held it down and said, "This is more indecent than being bare, for goodness sake! Don't bullfighters have capes with weights sewed in for windy days?"

"If you don't like it, don't wear it. Come on."

We cut across the key in the general direction of the water tower. It was heavy going, full of swamp and roots, vines and bugs. There was no wind and it was sweaty work. I broke off leafy twigs for us to use as fly whisks. I watched carefully for what I suspected we might find. When I saw it, I stopped abruptly. She held my arm tightly and we watched the slow fat coiling of a moccasin as it moved off into a tangle of black roots.

"Okay?" I asked her.

"I won't bother them if they won't bother me."

"When it's cold they get so sluggish you might step on one before you noticed it."

"Isn't it a *lovely* hot day, darling!"

At last I saw the green water of the bay through the trunks of the mangroves at the water's edge. I stepped carefully down into the mud between the tough exposed roots of the mangroves. Shallow mud flats extended perhaps three hundred yards to land that could be an island or a projection of the key we were on. Beyond it, across more water, I could see the south edge of the island where the water tower stood.

"Stay right behind me," I told her. "We'll walk across these flats. Scuff your feet with each step. If we come to an oyster bar, I'll circle it."

"Scuff my feet?"

"The sting rays sit on the mud and sand in shallow water in the hot months. If you should lift your foot and come down on one, he'd nail you."

"So I should bump the edge of one?"

"And he'll flap away, indignant, irritable, but without reprisal."

"If I see one I'll flap away too, like a seagull, buddy. Cawing."

On the way across the flats I saw a few stirrings in the mud ahead of me, and the roiled signs of flight. Once we were far enough out for the west wind to catch us, it was harder to see bottom and I went more slowly. An old granddaddy mullet sailed up out of the water ten feet to our left, making her gasp.

When we reached the south end of the first tip of land I looked ahead and saw that the water was deep enough for swimming.

"You're going to get that nice shirt wet," I told her.

"It might be more modest that way," she said.

"I somehow doubt the hell out of that."

"What do we aim for, boss?"

I studied the island. It was perhaps six hundred yards away. The water tower was definitely on that island, but I could see no break in the mangroves along the west or south shore line.

"We'll head up the side of it there and swim around that point and see what we can see."

We waded in carefully, shuffling our feet, and began swimming as soon as the water reached my waist. We had to buck a slow tidal current. The only unpleasant thing about it was its tendency to paste a long green slimy strand of seaweed across your face from time to time. The water was warm. I could feel more of the tension and pain being worked out of my muscles. I felt a slight weakness that came, I suspected, from hunger. After a long and steady pull I veered over to an area that looked shallow and tested it. It was up to my armpits. I could stand there by leaning into the steady current. I held her by the nape of the neck as she floated on her back, resting.

I looked down the length of her fondly. "Nothing modest about that shirt, girl."

"Hush now!"

"About the same effect as a coat of primer."

Six pelicans sailed by, twenty feet away, their wing tips a quarter-inch from the surface of the water. They ignored us. I explained to Peggy that they had been around before mankind had appeared to mess up the fishing, and they had several fairly good reasons to expect to be around after we had become history. She said they hadn't looked because they were too courteous to stare, which was more than she could say for the man of her choice.

We returned to the business of swimming. We rounded the point and I saw some hefty channel markers ahead. We swam along, parallel to the north shore of the island, and a big boathouse slowly came into view, with a big open boat visible within the white open framework and some skiffs tied alongside.

"There's a low platform thing on the far side of the boathouse," I told her.

"I see it."

As we swam to the low dock attached to the east side of the boathouse I read the name on the transom of the big open boat. The *Sandspur*. It rang a remote bell. I hoisted myself up out of the water and stood up. I saw a lovely quiet sweep of green lawn that went up a hill to the big old frame house that stood on the crest. Cocoanut palms stood tall and twisted by the wind. I saw frame cottages along the shore line. When I saw the sign hanging from the archway beyond the boathouse, I knew exactly where I was. Cabbage Key, the sign said.

I turned to give Peggy a hand up and she rejected it firmly. "I step right out of this water into a robe or a blanket, friend. Unless you can prove there aren't any people here."

A man in khakis and a T shirt came walking through the archway and onto the dock, wearing a look of inquiry. He was a trim sunbrown man in his middle years. He wore glasses with metal frames, and his expression was full of a mild good humor.

"Thought I heard somebody talking," he said. He looked across the water in all directions, obviously looking for a boat. "You folks anchored around the corner?"

"We didn't exaactly come by boat," I said. "I'm from Florence City. My name is Sam Brice. This is Peggy Varden. I guess you know Dr. Joe Arlington. He's talked about this place often."

He stepped down and shook hands with me. "I'm Larry Stultz," he said. "Joe is an old friend and customer." He stared with curiosity at Peggy who had lowered herself until only her eyes showed over the edge of the dock. "Won't you come ashore, Miss Varden?"

"She . . . she's not dressed for swimming, Mr. Stultz."

"If you've got anything I could cover myself with, I would certainly . . ."

"Of course! Of course!" he said, and went scurrying off. He went into the structure that adjoined the boathouse and came back in moments with a faded blue seersucker robe. He turned and stood with his back to us. I leaned down and gave Peggy a hand. She climbed up, wiggled out of the shirt and dropped it onto the dock with a sodden sound and gratefully hustled herself into the robe and belted it."

"Now I'm decent," she said.

When Larry turned with a polite smile of welcome, I said, "We had to leave a boat in a big hurry last night, about four miles out in the Gulf off LaCosta. We swam to shore and this morning we came across LaCosta and waded and swam here."

"Boat catch fire?" he asked mildly.

"No. It was just going to be . . . too unpleasant if we stayed aboard."

"Four miles is a good swim."

"There wasn't much choice, Mr. Stultz."

"Glad you made it all right," he said.

Peggy was frowning slightly as she stared at him. "My goodness, people arrive swimming and you act as if it

176

happened every day, Mr. Stultz."

He grinned at her. "I used to be in the advertising business in Chicago. My wife, Jan, and I have run this place as a vacation hideaway for ten years. After those two ways of making a living, Peggy, if there's anything left in this world that can startle me very much, I can't think right now what it could be. Let's go up to the house."

Jan, a slim, tanned, brisk and competent lady, took the event in stride, in exactly the same way Larry did. In spite of our protests, which perhaps were not very emphatic, we were given a big breakfast, the loan of dry clothing, a pack of cigarettes and a forty minute ride up to Boca Grande in the *Sandspur*. Larry explained that they had two boatloads of guests coming down from Sarasota to arrive in mid-afternoon and more guests to be picked up in Boca Grande before lunch. He had been planning, he said, to run to Boca for supplies anyway, and this just meant getting there a little earlier than he had planned. It was the quickest way to get us to a phone.

He docked the *Sandspur* just beyond the Pink Elephant, a small hotel at Boca Grande. I placed a collect call to Pat Millhaus from there. When I could hear him grumbling and threatening not to accept it, I told the operator to tell him it was an emergency.

"Pat?"

"Can't you afford a phone call, Brice?"

"Can you have this recorded so you can check it over if you have to?"

"What can you tell me that I should have . . ."

"Do you want to know who killed Sis and Charlie Haywood?"

I listened to a shocked silence, and then he said, "Let me get this thing hooked up."

After it began to beep at fifteen second intervals, I told him who to pick up, and where they might be found, and how fast he would have to move. When he tried to interrupt I yelled him down. I gave him descriptions as complete as I could make them. Peggy stood close to me, prompting me on points I had overlooked.

"Suppose it's a false arrest deal?" he complained.

"Damn it, Millhaus, I have proof. And if they get clear because you didn't budge off your fat tail, I'll make certain every newspaper in Florida gives you some big headlines you won't like."

"You can't talk to me like . . ."

I hung up on him. I knew he would move fast, but I did not know if it would be fast enough. I hadn't quite dared request that a car be sent after us. I ran the borrowed dime through the phone again and this time I made it collect to D. Ackley Bush.

"My dear boy, this is a horrid time of day to ask anyone to . . ."

"Ack?"

"Yes, Samuel."

"I have the Weber house guest with me. And we have all the answers, Ack. And if you can keep your mouth shut all the way back to Florence City, we might tell you the whole thing before even the sheriff knows it."

"Dear boy, you are now at the Pink Elephant?"

"Yes."

"I estimate the running time of my timid little machine to be fifty minutes. And I shall leave here in . . . ten."

It gave me an hour to prepare her for D. Ackley Bush, and tell her the part he had played in my life. She was prepared to adore him by the time he came clattering up in his little gray car.

"Do drive, Samuel. If I try to drive and listen, I shall roll us into a field. Glory be, what a handsome neighbor I had and didn't know it! You have a very good face, child. You two exude a sweet rapport. Beware of linking your future to this bonehead, dear girl. His great flaw is his desire to impress the world with his open, amiable stupidity, whereas we who love him know he is an almost excessively complex creature."

I drove. Peggy was beside me. There was no room for three in front. Ack rode in the back, but he leaned forward with an enduring intensity that kept his rosy old face suspended between us.

The story lasted longer than the trip. I turned in at my place. I had to break into the cottage. Peggy fixed iced tea. I located the extra key to my wagon, and changed into clothing that fit me. We sat on the porch with Ack and finished the story.

He shook his head slowly. "A dismal thing, children. A

sad, dirty, frightening thing. Utopia will never be possible until we have no more two-legged animals. Can they be bred out of the race?" He looked at Peggy and said gently, "Will you feel very bad about your step-sister, my dear?"

"I . . . I don't think so. She had me come down both summers not because she really needed me, Ack, but because it gave her a chance to pretend to herself there was something even a little bit normal about the way she was living. She lied to that poor Charlie Haywood. She was drunk most of the time. Yesterday afternoon was when she killed anything I might have felt for her."

"How?" Ack asked.

"She knew they had me, and they'd hurt me, and she didn't know what they were going to do to me; so she kept drinking so she would have an excuse she could tell herself. They had me in the main house then, and I heard Maurice raise his voice, telling her to get Sam into the house when he came. I yelled through a locked door to her, as loud as I could, 'Tell Sam to run! Tell him to bring help!' I know she heard me. They all did. Weber came in and cuffed me around and they put me out in that utility room then. You wouldn't know she was as drunk as she was, because she could walk and talk pretty well right up until the time she passed out, but she could have told Sam to run. She asked him in, so they could hit him."

"People better not hit you with this lady present," Ack said. "That welt over your ear looks nasty, Samuel. How do you feel?"

"As if I'd spent a full ten-hour day trying to stop Rick, Jimmy Brown and Allan the Horse."

"Gentlemen!" Peggy said firmly. We stared at her. "I have no comb, toothbrush, lipstick, money or bed to sleep in. No clothes, nothing. I slept in a sand pile last night. I'm waterlogged. If I start to yawn, I won't be able to stop. I'm not ready for any kind of official questioning. Somebody better do something about me before I start screaming and leaping."

I donated a shower and a bed. Ack volunteered to purchase all the items on the list she made out, and bring them back to the cottage. I headed for the Florence County Court House.

Chapter Eleven

MEMORY RETAINS only the sharpest images, the violences, the dramatics, the incongruities.

But I can remember a lot of the interminable questioning. T. C. Barley, the State's Attorney handled most of it. Pat Millhaus was there, and Deputy LeRoy Luxey and another deputy. Bunny Biscoe had wormed his way in, presumably on the basis of not releasing anything with the approval of Barley and Millhaus. Cal McAllen was there, with the worn, stunned look of a man who has been told he has something incurable. There were a couple of officials there I couldn't identify, and a court reporter tapping each word onto a stenotype tape. The Mahlers had been found in Lauderdale and were being brought back for questioning.

After I had been through all of it the first time, Barley kept taking me back to my initial suspicions, the beginnings of my investigation.

"You concealed an escaped convct?" he asked again.

"Yes."

"And if you had turned him in, Miss Gantry would now be alive? I am making the assumption she is dead, of course."

"Yes, I know that. I didn't know it would happen that way, but it did. And I'm going to have to learn to live with it."

"Mr. Brice, I have yet to get a satisfactory answer from you that is pertinent to one whole area of this investigation. You kept accumulating facts and rumors that would have been of great interest to Sheriff Millhaus, yet you did not come forward and tell him what you were learning. Why?"

I glanced at Pat's impassive Indian face. "I am not one of the sheriff's favorite people, Mr. Barley. He would have taken the smallest excuse to whip my skull and stick me onto one of his road gangs. I didn't care to take that chance."

"That's a goddam lie!" Pat roared. "My personal opinions don't come in at all. I tried everybody fair and equal in my job. He could have come to me. He's trying to cover up something, the way it looks to me."

"Well, Mr. Brice?" T. C. Barley said.

In the silence LeRoy Luxey cleared his throat in such a meaningful way that everybody looked at him. He licked his lips and swallowed, looking like a shy leathery child. He said humbly, "Maybe I shouldn't say one word on account I whipped this fella's head by myself, but it was an honest mistake he brung down on hisself. But he did get that little girl out of bad trouble. And I say fair is fair, no matter what it costs a man. If'n this Brice had come in here with his ideas, the sher'f would not listened at all. This sher'f would have jailed him for any small thing on account this sher'f hates Brice and tole me so hisself and has been dreaming on ways he could get Brice locked up so he could whip his head for him nine times a day, which he said to me in his own words."

"You're through!" Pat yelled at the small man.

Barley looked quietly amused. "Luxey," he said, "turn in your badge. It so happens I have an opening on my personal staff. I can use a man who believes that . . . fair is fair, no matter what it costs."

Luxey pointed a thumb toward Millhaus. "A job like that, Mr. Barley, what will it make me to him?"

"When you deal with him, Luxey, you will be representing me. And when you work in this county, you'll be working with him, not for him."

"I would surely like it just that way," LeRoy said.

Just as it began to look as though the top of Pat's head was going to blow off, the phone rang. We all knew that only that one call was authorized to come through. Millhaus listened for a long time, grunting infrequently, and finally said, "We'll put out the welcome sign. Thanks, Ed," and hung up.

"Got 'em!" he said. "I was dreadful scared they would split up, making it almost too tough to spot em, but Ed Howe and his people nailed them at the Tampa International just a while back, ten minutes before they got on an Eastern flight to New York. Their luggage has gone, but we'll have it grabbed at the other end and shot back. They're saying it's some mistake, which is to be expected. I guess they figured you and that girl drowned and they would have time to get out safe without splitting up, Sam."

He gave me a wide warm friendly grin that fooled nobody.

I remember very vividly the scene that evening in Pat Millhaus's office. By then Peggy had rested and had been questioned and was dressed in one of the glamorous summery outfits Ack had bought for her. (He had expanded the hell out of her simple list, labeling it all pre-wedding presents.)

T. C. Barley had us sit side by side off to the left on the leather couch against the wall where they would not see us as they were brought in. By then, of course, battalions of news people were milling around the halls and drinking beer out on the courthouse lawn in the warm dusk after the late afternoon rains.

They brought Ben in first—Benjamin Kelley he called himself—big, impassive, freckled, brutalized, wearing the attitudes of previous imprisonments.

"Do you know those people?" Barley asked, pointing.

He turned and stared at us. He was very good. I could detect absolutely no change of expression. "No sir," he said. "I don't know them."

"He shot and killed Captain Chase," Peggy said in a small but firm voice. "He carried me aboard the Sea Queen. Then he left in the rental car to drive it down to Naples to meet the other two."

"I don't know what the lady is talking about," he said.

They took him out and brought Marty in. Rafael Martino, he called himself. He looked undressed without his cigar.

When directed to look toward us, he didn't handle it quite as well as Ben Kelly had. His expression did not change, but his color paled to a bloodless gray and was suddenly oiled by sweat.

"I never saw these people in my life," he said in a husky whisper.

"He and Mr. Weber burned my hand," Peggy said. "The Mahlers can identify him and the other one too. He tried to . . . rape me aboard the boat."

"She's nuts," Marty said, but it carried no conviction. I remembered his certainty that things would go wrong, his contempt for amateur operations. Things could not have gone much more wrong.

Weber was last. And he was not a pro. He walked in arrogantly.

"It's about time you people did some explaining," he said.

"Do you know those people over there?"

He turned quickly and looked at us. "Hello, Maurice," Peggy said. He looked as if he had been sledged in the pit of the stomach. His mouth dropped open and his eyes rolled wildly. He took a half-step and I thought he was going to go down, but he caught his balance.

"Can't you say hello?" Peggy asked blandly.

In the silence you could sense the way his mind was racing around the small perimeter of the trap, looking for some gap, some tiny logical place just big enough to wiggle through.

"Hello, Peggy," he said at last in a ghastly voice. He had to acknowledge knowing her.

Peggy nodded at T. C. Barley. "It was his cute little plan to drown the three of us, just like he had the other two drowned, Mr. Barley."

"It didn't work very well, Mr. Weber, or whatever your name is," Barley said.

I suspect that for a few seconds he came very close to breaking completely, turning into a droning, helpless idiot. But he slowly gathered the small strength remaining to him and said, "I get to have a lawyer, don't I?"

"Before the indictment by the Grand Jury, yes."

"I got the money for a good one," he said.

"I think you'll need a good one," Pat Millhaus said, grinning like a raccoon.

In the end it was LeRoy Luxey who simplified the problems of the prosecution. He studied the transcripts of the statements made by Peggy and me and the Mahlers. He decided where a little persuasion might help. And he arranged, without authorization, a little soundproof time with Martino. There are those who claim that Martino has never been quite right, mentally, since being interviewed by LeRoy. It is a fact that for days he would scream at any sudden sound. But it cannot be denied that, in one sense, Luxey did him a favor. In return for his vast eagerness to assist the prosecution, he was given thirty years, as opposed to the death by electrocution awarded Weber and Kelly.

Lou Leeman, with top legal assistance, managed to trace Starr Development back to a series of dummy principals and fictitious addresses in a large city in Michigan, but there the trail was lost in an impenetrable tangle. When it was clear that Weber would die, Lou waited for the delayed exposure that would blow the lid off that city. But nothing happened. Nothing at all. Unless two curious things that happened indicate that the men who were to be exposed by the Weber documents had a second line of defense.

A safe was blown in the office of one of the most reliable lawyers in that city, a man who could not be reached or bribed. It was assumed to be a ludicrously amateur job because the safe-cracker had used so much soup he had not only blown the safe open on all four sides, but had atomized the contents, blown a wall down and broken windows in a three block area. No one was hurt and it was considered a miracle that the clumsy thief or thieves had escaped alive.

Ten days later there was an explosion in a bank vault in that same city. A charge placed in a safety deposit box had gone off. The young woman who had previously rented the box testified that she had received a hundred dollar bill in the mail, and then received a phone call telling her that if she would give up her box on such and such a day, she would get a second hundred. The box rental people at the bank said that the box was rented ten minutes after the girl gave it up, to a man so ordinary-looking they could give no helpful description of him, and who had given a false address. Explosive experts said that it had been a crudely shaped charge activated by a clockwork timing mechanism and apparently designed to exert maximum force on the next box to the left of the one containing the charge. The adjacent box was rented by a young contractor, a man of recognized probity. The blast turned the contents of his box to black confetti.

Operating on the basis of that kind of hunch that distinguishes top reporters from the pedestrian thousands, Lou interviewed the lawyer and the contractor and learned that each of them had agreed to hold a bulky envelope handed to them by a man named Maurice Bergamann who used to work at City Hall. They had each been receiving post cards four times a year which always said "Okay, M.B." If any four-month period had elapsed without such a card coming, they were to put their envelope in the hands of the F.B.I. Bergamann had been so plausible when he set it up that both men were astonished they had been part of the apparatus of a blackmail scheme. And both men were bitterly indignant that the planned destruction of the Bergamann documents had totally destroyed other papers of great importance to them.

In this way Weber was accurately identified as the missing Bergamann. By then he was awaiting execution, but he was curiously composed and confident. It was remembered later that he acquired this curious confidence after receiving a typewritten letter from the north. All incoming mail was read before it was turned over to the prisoner. Bergamann destroyed the letter after spending a large part of one day, reading it over and over.

The guard who had checked that letter was semi-literate. "It was just a lot of words," he said. "Like legal stuff. Pressures brought to bear in high places and stuff like that. It didn't say much of anything."

At any rate, when they came after Bergamann, he blandly inquired if they were bringing him his new reprieve, and they told him no, that they were now going to stop the world for a moment and let him off.

They say he kept bucking and jumping and yelling, "Wait! Wait!" They say it took four men to hold him. He kept yelling about naming names, and dates and places and amounts of money. In fact he did begin yelling names in a crazy, high, whinnying voice, but they were names nobody had ever heard of, so they wrestled him in, forced him into the chair and strapped him down. He kept yelling for everybody to wait, so that he had no chance to hear any part of the prayer being said. They gave him three jolts, pronounced him dead and rolled him out ready for a charity burial. Nobody wanted the body, and the lawyer had wound up with all the money he had saved out of his blackmail income by living cheaply.

But way back before the trial, before the state could assemble its case, it was essential to find some bodies.

That memory is the worst of all. That is the one I would like to discard, but it is lodged too firmly in my mind, all ready and waiting for those rare nights of nightmare.

Based on Martino's testimony, it looked as if it might be possible to locate the Renault. He thought they had run straight out from Horseshoe Pass for twenty-five minutes, approximately, before Weber-Bergamann had stopped the Sea Queen dead in the water. They had left the removable section of the rail back at the dock. The car was lashed down. It had been a close fit bringing it aboard easing it along the two planks between the dock and the deck. Martino said that when Ben Kelly had released the hand brake after it was untied, it had slipped away from them and gone smashing into the rail when the Sea Queen rolled in a trough. It had rolled back and gone over Weber's foot. He had been yelling and cursing and limping and telling them to grab the car and hold it, but on the next roll it had gone neatly through the space where they had removed the section of railing. The windows were up.

"It floated right side up for a hell of a long time," said the transcript of Marty's oral testimony. "Ben wanted we should ram it and sink it, but Maurie said to wait. About a foot of it was sticking out and in a little while you could just see the shiny top in the moonlight, floating kind of stern-heavy. Then it was just gone. I didn't see bubbles or anything where it had been. It just sank and Maurie got the boat started up and we came back and after a little while he turned the lights on. But that railing was a mess. All bent and splintered. And he was trying to think of what he'd tell Chase, who'd been sent up to Tampa on a goose chase to keep him out of the way."

It became an obsession with the local skin divers to find that car. We had a lot of windy weather and a series of bad thunder storms which hampered the search.

Two days after Peggy had gone back to Richmond, the weather was just right for a more efficient search method. The Gulf was like a dull blue mirror. I managed to wheedle myself aboard the big Coast Guard helicopter that took off a half-hour before noon, not realizing how many times I would wish that I had never had the impulse.

When we got out over the Gulf we could see the big fast launch standing by with cable and marked buoy aboard. The proposed search pattern was marked on the chart of the area. Assuming a half-hour running time at fifteen miles an hour, the plan was to start five miles out and make a sweep about three miles long, parallel to the shore line, turn 180 degrees and come back about a hundred to two hundred yards further out, dropping small bags of yellow marked dye in order to be sure of staying in the search pattern. The launch tagged along behind us after chasing off a few boats that wanted to join the party.

After experimenting with various altitudes, the pilot found that about three hundred feet gave us the best combination of range and visibility. With the sun overhead and the water exceptionally clear, we could see the pale sand bottom and the irregular patches of weed, and it seemed that we would not be able to miss seeing the small black car down there.

I lost count of the sweeps. My eyes began to burn with the continual strain of searching the bottom. A young Coast Guard man and I lay face down on the cramped cabin floor with the port door braced open, our chins out over the edge, the rotor blowing a deafening gale down

187

onto the backs of our heads. He had additional duty. Every time he was kicked in the leg, he had to drop a bag of dye.

"Bingo!" the kid beside me screamed. I looked where he pointed and saw it at once. It looked incongruous. It was in the biggest empty parking lot in the world, sitting placidly on its wheels.

We dropped down and circled it. Below a hundred feet it was much more difficult to see.

The pilot suddenly became enraged when he found he could not make radio contact with the launch. Little gusts of wind had begun to riffle the water and black clouds were climbing up out of the west; I estimated we would have another forty minutes of direct sunlight. The receiver on the launch had conked out. The men on the launch ignored our attempts to indicate the spot and made expansive helpless shrugging motions. The pilot was filled with helpless fury.

I went to him and spoke into his ear over the rotor noise. "Take this thing low and drop me and I'll swim to the launch and you can guide us in."

I stripped down to my shorts. He brought it right down to the water and held it steady and even tilted it to make it easier to dive out of the doorway into the water made turbulent by the captive hurricane of the rotor vanes. I swam to the launch and was helped aboard.

"Damn, stupid, lousy radio," the launch captain said.

"We spotted it. He'll hang directly over it at three hundred feet and you come in on it by watching which way he points the nose of that thing. When you're over it, he'll do a big dip as a signal to drop your hook."

"What's the bottom?"

"Sand, it looks like."

"Fathometer says we got seventy feet here, and I got only a hundred feet of anchor line. There's one hell of a tidal drift and it won't hold in sand. Barney, break out that float and cable and get it all ready. Bus, you get set with the end of that cable to go on down when he gives the signal."

As Bus, a hearty bruiser, got himself ready, I saw the extra fins and face mask and said, "Maybe he can use some help. Mind if I go down too?"

"This is straight diving, no tanks," he said.

"I've been a lot deeper a lot of times."

He nodded. I adjusted the fin straps and the mask and stood on the bow beside the one called Bus. When we got the signal we lowered ourselves into the water, upended and went down. He had the weight of the cable to help him, but I had both arms free, so we made about the same time. The water color changed from gold to a clear pale green, to increasing depths of green. I saw the car in the murk off to the right and angled down that way, with Bus close by. We each caught the rear bumper and pulled ourselves down. I saw that it would help him to be able to use both hands, so I caught him around the waist and held him there. The Florida license plate looked insane. He threaded the snap end of the cable around the rear axle, brought it up and took a turn around the sturdy bumper brace before snapping it back onto itself. He gave it a tug then sprung up and out of sight. I should have followed him. I worked my way around the car, sensing I was nearing the end of my endurance. There was enough sun so that I saw her in a dark green luminous light. She was behind the wheel. There was a shadow beyond her. The safety belt—about which I had kidded her, was latched firmly across her. She was slumped against the window, looking out at me, her mouth open, her eyes open, her black hair floating still and wild in the endless silence of the flooded car. For that moment I cannot forget, her face was inches from mine, separated by the glass I could not see.

I went up too fast at first, then slowing myself, releasing air from my lungs as I went up. It was a winding silver thread under the compression, turning into bubbles as I neared the surface. I came up through green, through gold, breaking out into the world of sun and sanity. The big red and white plastic float rested on the quiet water. I sucked the warm clean air deeply into my lungs. Off in the west I saw a short fat blue dagger of lightning bang down into the dark water under the clouds.

The helicopter was floating off toward the mainland.

"Thanks for the help," Bus said. "What kept you?"

"I wanted to see if they were in the car."

189

"The guy said they were in the car, dint he?"

"I wanted to make sure."

"You don't look so good, fella. The crabs been working them over?"

"The windows were closed."

"Me, on a thing like that, I take the guy's word for it."

We turned and ran for shelter, and the sun was gone under the thunderheads by the time we got in.

I heard later how they worked it, how they recovered the car. I didn't care to see any part of it. They went out in a work boat and recovered the buoy and bent the cable around a winch and plucked the tin coffin off the floor of Gulf. When they brought it to the surface they put another line on it and used a boom to swing it aboard. It leaked water throughout the long trip back to the Florence City Municipal Pier, and the upright bodies sagged in a boneless way as the water level dropped inside the little sedan.

I attended Sis's funeral. All the Gantrys looked through me and beyond me, never at me.

After the funeral, until it was time to fly up to Dayton to be married, I worked like a horse, not only catching up on everything, but also breaking a kid in on the work so that he could at least handle the most routine things while I was gone. And I had begun to think about an office of my own, and maybe getting into actual adjusting work for some of the smaller companies and maybe expanding my area a little.

There isn't much more to tell. I brought my bride back. We used the *Lesser Evil* for a honeymoon that consisted of all the hot weekends in September and October, until the first chill of the winter season came down out of the north. We camped out on empty beaches, snug under all the stars.

We had our own private honeymoon habit of swimming naked in the warm shallow sea, and finding that buoyant incomparable love in the shallows whenever there was no surf. She would ask me solemnly if I thought there was very much danger of our toes becoming webbed.

That brings me to the best memory of all. It was a September night on LaCosta Key, a night of a full moon. She was curled beside me under the mosquito bar, but I could not sleep. There was enough of a west wind to keep the bugs away, so I slipped out quietly and walked down to the edge of the water.

I began to think of the *Sea Queen*. They had not yet given up looking for her at that time. I thought of her out there in the deeps. Maybe she had opened up enough so that the currents moved through her, so that Charity and Captain Stan Chase were at that moment doing an infinitely slow dance down there where the moonlight would never reach, taking a full five minutes for each bow, each random pirouette.

It struck me with horrid force that four of us could be down there, in that black minuet, touching, turning, spinning with slow rotten grace.

It was a moment of nightmare so real that I could not believe in that moment that my Peggy existed. I turned to go back to her and saw her coming slowly down the slope of the beach toward me, reaching a sleepy hand in a woman's habit to pat her shining hair, moving toward me in slender, silvered loveliness.

"I lost you," she said in a grumpy sleepy voice. She stood close and peered up into my face. "That's a strange expression."

"I started thinking about . . . where we might have been tonight, and what it's like down there. And suddenly all this didn't seem real."

She put her arms strongly around me and held herself tightly against me. "Oh, darling, it's real. It's very real."

"It just made me feel strange."

"You come with me," she said. She took my hand and we went back to the blankets and lifted the edge of the mosquito bar and crawled under.

"I'll show you how real it is," she said.

And she gave of herself with a completeness, a tenderness and a yearning strength that brought my world back into focus, back to sweet reality.

After it had ended, we shared one cigarette in that earthy and comforting silence which only love can create. She did not have to ask me what she had done for me. She knew.

191

After I reached out to stub the cigarette into the sand she sighed and took my hand and held it against her trim stomach and said, "Do you think he shows yet?"

"He won't show for months." (He was what you could call prominent when we had to testify at the murder trial in March.)

"Do you think he'll have fins?"

"What!"

"Considering what you've put me through, mister, the little son of a gun will probably have gills, fins, scales and he'll love worms."

"You've carefully concealed your reluctance."

She nestled her head against my throat and said comfortably, "I've hated every living minute of it. Mmmm. Seems as if every time I turn around, slosh, there I am flat on my back in the surf. Golly, I'm learning all the constellations, though. But in the daytime, I think you ought to give me a chance to put on my sunglasses. You know, darling, some women actually rub their faces with sandpaper as a beauty treatment, and if sand helps, I ought to have the most beautiful . . ."

"Shut up and go to sleep. I love you."

"Yes sir," said my bride.

In a little while I was able to reach down and pull up the sheet without putting a hitch in her deep and regular breathing. I admired Orion's belt for a little while and then slid down into sleep, grinning like a fool, thinking something about the longest way around being the shortest way home.